The NEWLYWEDS

Natasha Tsarina

Pillow Book Media Pte. Ltd
Singapore Business Registration 201316808N
©Pillow Book Media 2018

ISBN-10 981-11-5045-1
ISBN-13 978-981-11-5045-6 (pbk)
eISBN-10 978-981-11-5046-3
eISBN-13 981-11-5046-X (eBk)

ALL information and comments in this book are true and complete to the best of the author's knowledge. All recommendations are made for general information only, without any implied or express warranty on the part of the author or Pillow Book Media as to the suitability or fit for purpose of the recommendations. To the extent permitted by law, the author and publisher disclaim any implied or express liability in connection with this book and the use of the information herein.

Typeset | diacriTech Pvt Ltd
Editor | Doris Wai
Cover design | George Mayer/Shutterstock.com

Contents

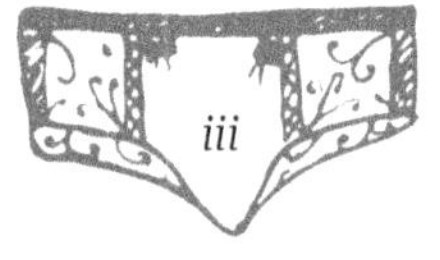

Chapter 1

huket International airport was a beehive of activity. There were tourists and locals everywhere and Cindy couldn't see her parents. Looking around for something to stand on, she saw a wooden bench to her right and put down her suitcase next to it, before climbing up on it.

She slowly turned around to see if she could spot them, but they were nowhere to be seen. She got down again and sighed. She thought for a minute and then decided to go outside. Maybe they were driving in circles waiting for her to come out? She had left her mobile phone in the ladies room at Zurich airport, and couldn't call them.

Outside, the humidity in the air was horrible. It felt like someone had put a hot wet towel over her face. The cool air of the Alps had been great, even though it became bitterly cold during the winter. Cindy lit a cigarette and attempted to listen to the people chatting away around her.

On the island of Ka Thai where Cindy had grown up, the dialect was different and some of the words that sounded the same meant completely different things. That, plus the fact that she had spent the last five years of her life in Switzerland had resulted in her losing touch with some of the dialects and that made it even harder to put colloquial words into context. After stubbing out her cigarette, she went back inside the waiting area.

"Cindy, Cindy!"

She turned and saw her mother making her way through the crowd. Her blonde hair was a head above everyone else's and when she finally reached Cindy, she hugged her daughter tight.

"My baby girl, how are you? Where were you?"

She spoke into her mother's neck. "I came out and I didn't see you, so I went outside for a smoke."

Her mother let go of her and took her face in her hands. "I missed you so much."

"Where is Dad?"

"He is buying newspapers."

"Again?"

Her mother smiled at her. "You know how he is."

Her father loved to read and whenever he was in town, he would buy all the newspapers and magazines he could get his hands on as there was no newsstand on the island of Ka Thai where he lived.

"Speaking about him, here he comes."

Cindy saw her father making his way through the crowd. He was carrying a plastic bag in each hand and she could see tons of newspapers and magazines sticking out. When he reached his daughter, he handed both bags to his wife and hugged her.

"My precious daughter, how are you? Let me take a look at you."

He let go of her and stood back. "You are not the same girl I dropped off at the airport five years ago. You are a woman now."

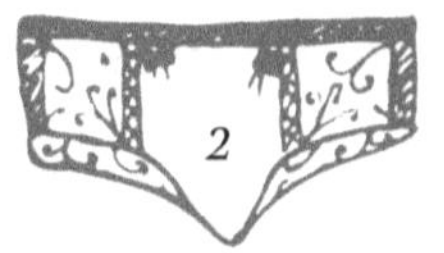

"She better be, especially since she is getting married tomorrow," said her mother.

Cindy wasn't upset that her soon-to-be husband, Tom wasn't there to meet her. She wanted to be alone with her parents. She would spend the rest of her life with him and for now, all she wanted to do as she wanted to seize the moment and catch up on old times with them before her big day.

"Let's go," said Ben, and took his precious bags of newspapers and magazines from his wife.

Cindy put her arm around her mother and picked up her luggage. It took them a while to make their way out of the airport and to the parking lot. When they were on the highway heading down to where their speedboat was moored, her mother told her everything about the ceremony.

"I've planned most of the details with Tom's mother and we have everything ready. The ceremony will be being held on the beach, followed by a dinner and drinks at the hotel."

"That's great! Thanks, Mum! I wouldn't know what to do if not for your help. Enough about me. How is business back at home?"

"Fantastic, better than we had expected. The investments we made have paid off and the tourists seem to like the newly renovated premises."

"That's great. I can't wait to get started, it's time for you to relax after all the hard work you have put in and let my new husband and I take care of the hotel."

Tula looked at her daughter and smiled. She was such a beautiful and sweet daughter. Tula had met Ben in 1989 when she went backpacking around the islands. At the time, Thailand

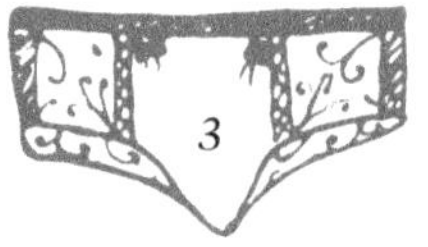

was not really on the map as far as tourism went, and the islands were still untouched. Ben had been working in his father's bungalow hotel, and they had fallen in love at first sight.

Things were tough at the beginning of the relationship. Ben's parents were getting on in years and thought that the Caucasian woman from the cold country far away was not right for their son. Moreover, she didn't speak their language and could not communicate with them even though their son could since he had picked up English from the tourists. The young couple did all they could to convince them otherwise. Tula also picked up Thai quickly and his parents eventually accepted her into the family. They asked her how it was to grow up in Finland and if they had polar bears on the streets. She had laughed and said no, and where she was from, Helsinki, was a big and modern city.

They were concerned that she would one day want to return to her country and either leave their only son or take him with her. What would they do then? She promised them that she loved Ka Thai too much to ever leave it.

A year later, they were married and Cindy was born a few months soon after. The young family worked hard in his parents' hotel and Cindy went to school in the small town.

Cindy was fourteen when a tragedy happened. She was playing with some friends and heard a commotion at the beach. One of the boys she was with climbed up a tree and saw the waves approach. They all ran up into the hills and as far into the jungle they could and stayed there for several hours. When they came down again, there was nothing left of the town.

Ben and Tula had gone to Phuket that morning and luckily, they had been away when the tsunami hit Ka Thai. Cindy's

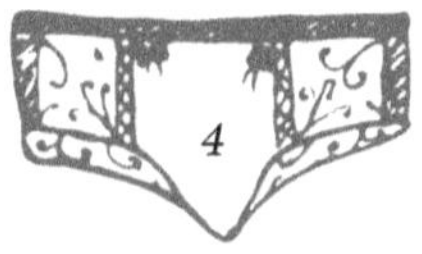

grandparents were cleaning the bungalows on the beach and had been swept away. By the time her parents came back, their bodies had found and were buried in mass graves along with hundreds of others.

Ben and Tula had sat down at the very spot where the reception's building once stood and had been reduced to mud and sand. Few structures were still standing and the smell of rotting bodies and fish was horrible. They thought they had lost their daughter and when she came running towards them along the beach, they both cried.

Ben's father had owned the land and when he died, Ben inherited it. With the help of some neighbors, he rebuilt the hotel and the bungalows. Things took a turn for the better with the foreign aid money given post-disaster and with that, the transport and infrastructure in Ka Thai were improved. The harbor and port were expanded so the island could receive more tourists.

The couple struggled to keep the hotel open in the first two years and there were times when they thought about selling it. However, Tula's *sisu*—a Finnish word for stoic determination, resilience and hardiness—kept them going. By 2008, their hard work had paid off and they managed to get their hotel running full house every day, throughout the year.

When Cindy turned eighteen, she told her parents she wanted to attend a hotel management school. Both Tula and Ben were pleasantly surprised. They had wanted their only daughter to take over the business but did not want to pressure her into doing so. While they thought that the young woman should decide what she wanted to do with her life, they were secretly worried that

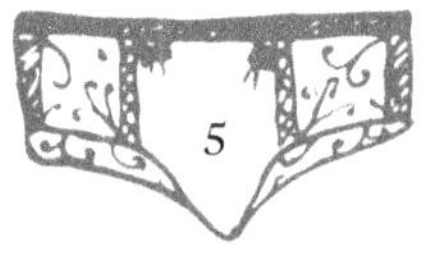

she would want to move away from the island. With a close friend's recommendation, Ben decided to send her to the best hospitality school in Switzerland. Five years later, she graduated second in her class and was ready to take over her parents' hotel in the little island of Ka Thai.

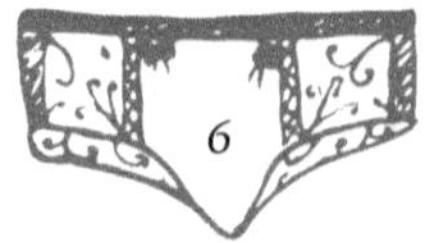

Chapter 2

"She is one hot dish, you know," said Mike enviously.

"Put that thought down and stop having sexual fantasies about my future wife," said Tom, and gave his friend another beer.

They were sitting outside his parents' house up in the hills. The sun had set several hours ago and on the table in front of them were several empty beer bottles and two shot glasses. The sound of the night was all around them—the chirping of insects, music coming from the bars and restaurants in the town and somewhere, a car horn could be heard.

It felt almost surreal to Tom that he would be married the following day and finally be living with Cindy. They had known each other for as long as he could remember. She had been his first kiss, and he her's. They had played and cried together on the beach and in the jungle. He was the one who had climbed the tree that horrible day and saw the waves come in, and he still remembered how he had comforted her after that tragic disaster. When she went to Switzerland he had cried for days. It was like a part of his body was missing, like as if it had been torn away and he could neither breathe, sleep nor eat. There was a hollow space in the pit of his stomach that only grew emptier each day.

When Tom's parents decided that he was going to America to study six months later, he was happy and sad at the same time for there was nothing he wanted more than to be with Cindy. Everything around him reminded him of her presence, but he had to focus on his studies instead. Before he left, he and his parents went over to Cindy's parents and it was decided that the young couple would get married upon their graduation. When he called Cindy and told her the news, she cried tears of joy.

Tom took out his wallet and looked at a photo of Cindy inside it. Her icy blue eyes and black hair made her stand out in a crowd. He then reminded himself of the few occasions that he had seen her in a bikini over the years and when he had come home, he had jerked off at the memory of her full boobs and round ass. The fact that she was slightly taller than him never did bother him one bit and if anything, he couldn't be more proud that she had inherited her mother's lithe body.

"What if Cindy has fucked some guy over there? Then she won't be a virgin," said Mike.

"She wouldn't do that. She loves me."

"Mm, sure she does. But think about it, she's thousands of miles away, and she is young and hot. Some guy must have tried to make a move on her. What if she was a little drunk or just plain horny? You never know what might happen."

"Oh, shut up! Not all women are like the sluts you hang out with."

"What?" Mike took a drink of his beer and looked away.

"I know you go down to the red light district and hang out in the strip bars. I bet that you have tried one of those lady boys."

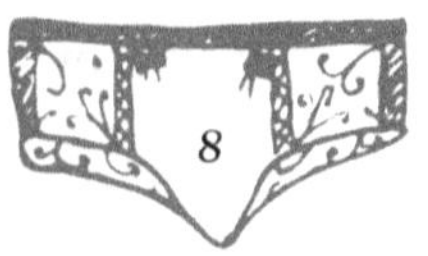

8

Mike cleared his throat and took another sip from his beer.

"See, I knew it. How was it? Did you like sucking cock?" jabbed Tom.

"Look. I didn't and I never will. I love pussy too much for that."

"OK, then stop talking about my future wife in that manner."

"I'm sorry. It's just that I've seen how the women in town behave with the tourists and it's plain nasty. Anyway, are you guys going on a honeymoon?"

"No, we are taking over her parents' hotel. Ben and Tula have decided to retire."

"Why? They are not even sixty."

"I guess they have had enough of work. The tsunami took a toll on them and they have worked day and night since then to make the hotel what it is today."

"So, what's their plan? Will they move to Finland? They say polar bears walk the streets there."

Tom laughed. "No, you idiot. They don't. Haven't you seen the house they have built across the street from the hotel?"

"OK, that makes sense. Your in-laws will stay there so they can keep an eye on you two, making sure you don't drive the hotel into bankruptcy."

"Fuck you! Cindy is smart and she knows about hotel management. I guess they just want to be around. They told us that they are moving into their new house on Monday and will officially hand over the reins of the hotel then. So, we only have the weekend to get ourselves up to speed on all the ins and outs of the hotel and what the bookings look like for this season."

"Shit, that sucks. You don't even get time off to fuck your new wife."

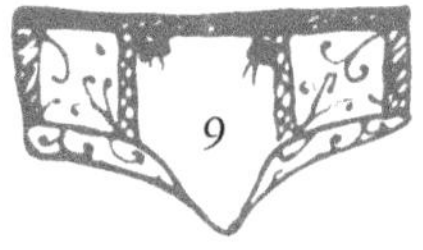

Tom glared at his friend. "Tell me, again how did it feel to fuck your first lady boy?"

"All right. Let's drop the subject. I'm sorry."

Mike and Tom continued to drink and talked late into the night. It was their version of a bachelor party—two friends talking, drinking and watching the tranquil night sky.

Later that night when Mike had gone home, Tom made some tea and looked at Cindy's photo again. He had been worried about her meeting someone else in college. This had haunted his dreams and he had silently prayed that she hadn't already lost her virginity to someone else. After all, he had not been so well behaved himself when he met Melanie in his second year of college. She was from Philadelphia and was in one of his classes. She liked to wear miniskirts and tight tops. Like most undergraduates, she smoked and drank a lot, and most of all, she was a flirt. She loved to tease the guys and get them all hot and horny for her. She tried to seduce Tom a number of times, but he simply ignored her. It wasn't that he didn't find her attractive. She was, in a slutty kind of way, but he had already made a promise to the love of his life and he had meant to keep it. However, it sure seemed like lust had other plans.

It happened on a rainy night in February. Tom had been invited to a party at a friend's house. Back in Thailand, he seldom had alcohol. His parents didn't drink and neither did Cindy, so there was no reason for him to do so. But in Kansas, most of his friends either literally drank their lives away or smoked an insane amount of weed.

Tom was on his third beer when Melanie walked in. She was dressed in a long trench coat and when she took it off, all the men in the room stopped talking. She was wearing a white cocktail dress with thin straps over her shoulders. Her makeup was perfect

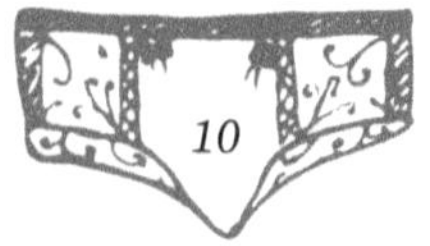

10

and her high heels simply further accentuated her impossibly long legs. The dress was wrong for the time of year, but no one gave a shit. Her eyes were fixed on Tom and she walked over to him with her hips swinging, one foot in front of the other. Before he knew it, she was so close to him that he could feel her C-cup breasts touching his chest as she breathed into his ear.

"Hi, handsome. I would like to have some delicious Thai takeaway."

Tom kept his cool and replied, "I believe there's a Thai restaurant two blocks down."

"Mm, I know, but the thing is … I need it fresh, right of the cooker, so to say."

He swallowed hard and drank some of his beer, buying himself some time to think of a witty response. He finally muttered, "Sorry, can't do it."

"I see. Well, I shall see you later."

She gave him a long look before walking off and Tom's eyes were fixated on the sight of her round ass. He then went back to his friends who gave him a hard time for rejecting a smoking hot kitten.

After a couple more drinks, Tom decided it was time to leave as he had morning classes the next day. By then, it was pouring outside and he didn't have an umbrella. He stood alone in the doorway wondering about his chances of getting a taxi. After a while, he decided to walk back instead since the bar only four blocks away from his place.

Two blocks down, a car drove up next to him and the window rolled down.

"Do you need a lift?"

He turned his head and saw Melanie in the car. "No, I am fine."

11

She laughed. "Don't be stupid, I won't bite. Get in or you will catch a cold."

Tom hesitated for a minute, and then decided it was better to take up her offer than to become sick. Besides, what could happen? It was warm inside the car and he could smell her intoxicating perfume.

"Where do you live?"

He pointed. "Up there, two blocks from here."

They drove in silence and when they were almost at his place, he stuck his hand in his pockets, looking for his keys. They were gone.

"What's wrong?" she asked.

"I think I have lost my keys."

Does your neighbour have a spare set?"

"No. Shit, I am so stupid."

"Don't worry. We can go back to my place, and then you can come back tomorrow to see if you've dropped it on the streets."

Tom wanted to decline her offer but decided against it when he checked the clock on the dashboard. It was already a quarter to four. He sighed. "OK, fine. Your place it is then."

"Great. And just so you know, I will behave."

He took a quick look at Melanie and saw that she had a grin on her face.

Her place was a ten-minute drive from his and when they finally got inside, he found himself in a neat two-bedroom apartment. There was a sofa and a TV at one corner and a dinner table by a window looking out onto the street. On the walls were pictures of Melanie with her family and friends.

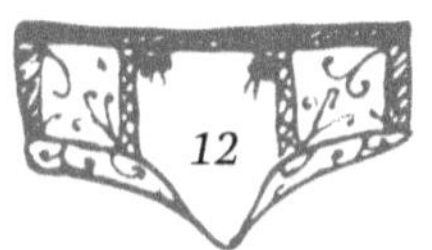

"You can sleep on the sofa," she said before going into her bedroom.

Tom took off his wet coat and hung it on a hook by the door, before taking off his shoes. Melanie came back shortly carrying a pillow and a blanket.

"Here you go, there is a draft coming in from the window at this time of the year and it can get a bit chilly in here."

"Thanks and good night."

"Night."

After making sure that she had closed the bedroom door, he removed his pants and sweater and hung them on the chairs next to the dinner table before lying down on the sofa. Tom immediately felt a strong gust of wind hitting his face. He turned around and pulled the blanket over his head. It didn't take long before he fell asleep.

He was suddenly jolted awake by a sensation he couldn't quite comprehend. He felt something wet and warm around his cock and looked down. Melanie was kneeling on the floor and her head was bobbing up and down. His cock was sliding in and out of her mouth and she had her eyes closed.

"Hey, what the hell?"

She looked up at him, but didn't stop. Instead, she put a finger on his lips and began to stroke his shaft while sucking him. Tom was about to push her away when he felt his balls contract. An involuntary moan escaped from his mouth and then he heard a swallowing sound, followed by a loud slurp.

"Wow, that was great," said Melanie while licking her lips.

"What have you done?"

"Oh, don't tell me you didn't like it, I know you did and by the way, you need to jerk off more often. It's not healthy to go for so long without coming."

"What the fuck are you talking about?"

He quickly sat up and pulled the blanket over his still-erect cock. Melanie was standing naked and looking down at him. Her boobs were rounder than he had imagined and she had perky pink nipples. Her pussy was shaved and she had a small tattoo of a dolphin on one hip.

"You just shot the biggest load I have ever tasted. It was enormous. Anyway, good night and sleep tight."

He watched her leave with her hips swinging and her perfect ass in full view. He spent the rest of the night laying in the darkness, deep in thoughts. He had just received the first blowjob in his life. It was a fantastic feeling but he had cheated on Cindy, and she must never find out.

Back to reality, Tom took a sip from his tea and looked at Cindy's photograph. He started to trace the outline of her lips with his fingers as he pictured her lips stretched around another man's shaft. To his surprise and his horror, he found himself with a hard-on.

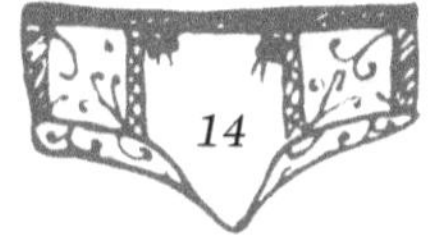

Chapter 3

indy and her parents were up early the next morning preparing for the ceremony and dinner party. The monks arrived at the wedding venue in the morning to bless the couple. When Tom arrived, he found his wife all dressed up in a traditional dress.

"Honey, you look beautiful," he gushed.

"Thank you, and you look very handsome."

They then left their parents to mingle with the guests and took a stroll along the beach as they indulged in their private moment. It was too early for the tourists to be awake and they had the white sand to themselves. Cindy took Tom's hand and he gave her a quick peck on the cheek.

"You missed graduation," he said.

"I know, but it was important to me and my parents that I fly out as soon as possible. Anyway, the graduation is just another ceremony and an excuse for everyone to get wasted after that."

Tom went back to that day when his father had told him that he would not be able to attend the graduation ceremony as he needed him to help out back at home. He was disappointed as he was very much looking forward to the ceremony and when he called Cindy to tell her about the bad news, she had told him that he should respect his father's wishes. It was then that he realized how much she had matured while studying overseas.

"What about your diploma?"

"They will send it to me by post."

"So, are you ready for this?"

Cindy giggled. "Of course I am. What about you?"

She stopped and looked him in the eyes. She loved this man more than anyone else in the world.

"I am but I am nervous."

"About?"

He looked down and brushed some sand off his foot. "I guess I am not sure if I will live up to your expectations as a husband."

Cindy looked surprised. "Why wouldn't you? You are a wonderful man and a fantastic person. I bet that you will make a great father to our children."

That made him smile. He had always wanted children and at least four of them. "I hope you are right."

"Don't be silly. C'mon, let's go back. Those monks are arriving any minute and we have to go to the Wat after that."

The Wat was a Buddhist temple and when couples got married, it was customary for them to make a donation so as to ensure luck and prosperity would follow them through their marriage.

The ceremony went as planned and about fifty people showed up to celebrate the couple's union. Mike was the master of ceremony and Cindy had been a bit worried when Tom told her that he wanted his friend to do so. After all, he was well known for being a drunkard and womanizer, and by the end of the

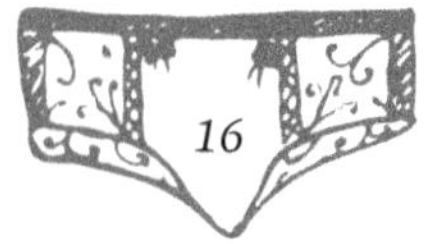

ceremony, even Tom was secretly surprised that Mike had pulled off the job.

Cindy and Tom's fathers also made short speeches thanking the guests and wishing the newlyweds well. When the dinner was almost over, the young couple retreated to their room.

Cindy sat down on the bed and took off her shoes. She massaged her feet for a few minutes and let out a huge sigh of relief, "This is it. We are now husband and wife."

Tom hung his shirt over a chair and turned around. "Yeah, we are. I have waited so long for this moment."

She indicated with her hand for him to come over and when he was standing in front of her, she slowly unzipped his pants. As they dropped to the floor, she looked up at him and smiled. "I have so long waited for this."

His manhood was rock hard and he watched as Cindy began to kiss his shaft: her lips, warm and moist against his skin. He closed his eyes and when she took him in her mouth, he sighed.

Cindy bobbed her head up and down, slowly at first and then more quickly. She felt a bit insecure, but didn't want her husband to know that she had no idea what she was doing. She had only seen him naked once and that was when they were teenagers. Back then, she had only caught a glimpse of his dick and had then quickly turned away. Looking up, she stole a look at his face and saw that his mouth was half open and his eyes closed. She was glad that he seemed to be enjoying himself. But while she ran her tongue over and around his cockhead, she couldn't help but think about another man—a man who made her pussy wet.

She had met Klaus at a café in the small town where the university was located. The streets were narrow and during winter, the snow piled up high along the house walls. There wasn't anything much in the area except for a church, several cafés, a few bookshops and some supermarkets. A short street with three bars was where the students hung out during the weekends. All three bars played the same music, charged the same prices and it was just a question of where your cool friends were hanging out.

She had been out shopping before her afternoon classes and had taken refuge from the snow and wind in the little café. After ordering a coffee and a pastry, she sat down at a table for two in the back. She started to flip through the pages of a magazine she had bought earlier and didn't notice the young man sitting down at a table opposite her until he stood right next to her.

"Hi, excuse me. Could I have the sugar, please?" he asked as he pointed to the small container on the table.

"Yeah, sure." she replied, not really paying attention to the man.

"Thank you."

Moment passed and she only saw his face when she took a bite from her pastry and happened to look away from the magazine. He was dressed in a dark blue suit, and had dark brown hair and an angular face. She guessed he was in his early thirties. A coat hung over the chair next to him and he was reading the local paper. Suddenly he looked up and their eyes met. Cindy looked away and felt herself blushing. She had never met anyone with emerald green eyes that were as striking as his. She went back to reading her magazine but every so often, she would steal a glance at him. He did not seem to be aware and continued reading as he

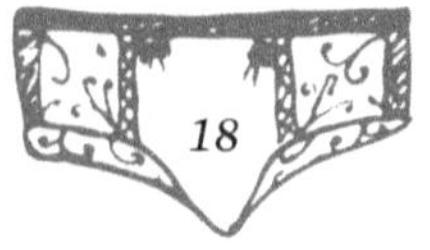

18

drank his coffee. When he was done, he stood up and collected his coat and a briefcase. When he saw her looking at him, he smiled. "Bye, and thanks for the sugar."

"You're welcome. Bye."

She watched through the windows as he turned right and walked up the street to the town centre.

"Be careful, young lady."

Cindy turned around. The woman who had served her earlier had finished cleaning the table where the man had sat, and she came over to Cindy's table.

"That was Klaus. He is a handsome man, but a total heartbreaker."

"Oh, I hardly noticed him," lied Cindy.

"Of course you didn't, my dear. But he noticed you and you can be sure he will come by here again to look for you."

"Why would he?"

She used a dirty cloth to wipe the remaining pastry crumbs onto the floor. "Because he likes young women, like you."

"I have a boyfriend back home."

"It makes no difference to him. He will get what he wants."

"Well, he can't have me."

The woman gave her a sad smile. "So you say. More coffee?"

"Yes, please."

Cindy spent another hour in the café. She saw that it had stopped snowing and decided it was time to make a move. She got up and spoke to the woman behind the counter.

"Thank you for earlier. Have a nice day."

"You are welcome. Remember what I said earlier about Klaus. Stay away from him, young lady."

As she stood on the sidewalk, Cindy pulled her coat close to her and put on her hat, which she had kept in her coat pocket. It might have stopped snowing, but it was still freezing and the wind was tugging at her hair. She started to make her way to the university by walk. It was way past lunchtime and there were only a few people on the streets. A couple of cars whizzed past her as she walked gingerly on the snow that covered the sidewalk. She was only a block away from her dormitory when someone walked up from behind her and tapped her on the shoulder. She almost slipped and to hold on to a lamp-post.

"Watch out!"

Cindy turned and saw Klaus standing next to her. "What are you doing?"

"I work just down the street and wanted to say hi when I saw you walking past the building."

Cindy let go of the lamp-post. She saw he was without his suit jacket and that he was shivering. "I see. Hi."

Klaus wrapped his arms around his body and rubbed his shoulders. "Can we go inside? It's kind of cold out here."

"I'm sorry but I have to go. I have class in half an hour."

"Oh, so you are a student at the university?"

"Yes, it was nice meeting you again."

He took out his wallet and gave her a card. "Call me."

He then smiled and walked away. Cindy watched him for a minute until he disappeared around a bend.

His name was Klaus Lutz and he was an architect. She turned the card over but there was no contact number on it. Running late for her classes, she stuffed it in her coat pocket and walked as fast as she could back to her room to pick up her assignments.

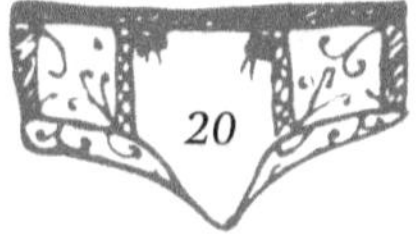

20

"Hi, Chantell," she called when she walked in.

"I am in the kitchen. Do you want something to drink?" asked Cindy's roommate.

"No, I'm fine, just picking up some stuff."

Chantell came out from the kitchen and leaned against the door post whilst wiping her hands with a small towel. "How's the weather outside?"

"Cold and windy. What are you up to?"

"Nothing much. I don't have class until evening."

Cindy went into her room and got what she needed before walking back to the living room. Before leaving, she turned around and tried to ask in a casual tone. "Do you know a guy named Klaus Lutz? Tall, brown hair, good-looking."

Chantell was twenty-three, single and liked to party a lot. She was out most weekends while Cindy preferred to stay at home with a book or watch TV.

"Maybe. Is he an architect?"

"Yeah."

"I don't know him personally, but I have seen him around town. He's got quite a reputation. Why do you ask?"

"I met him twice today. The second time round, he gave me his card and asked me to call him."

"Oh la la! Cindy has a date. What would Tom say about that?"

Cindy laughed. "Don't be stupid. I am not going on a date with him."

"So, why the question?"

"Curiosity, I guess."

"Mm, I see. Well, I usually see him with a new woman every weekend, so be careful."

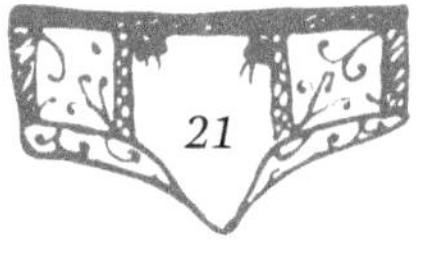

21

Cindy stuck her tongue out at her friend and left. She ran down the stairs and across the campus, barely making it in time for class.

Chantell went back to the kitchen and finished washing the dishes. Just the thought of Klaus made her wet. She had met him a few weeks earlier and had ended up in bed with him the very night. She has a healthy appetite for sex and the man's cock was impressive to say the least. It was big and rock-hard, and she had loved every inch of it. While Klaus himself was quite the looker, his manhood was phenomenal, and she wasn't about to share that detail with Cindy, even though she was sure her friend would never cheat on her boyfriend.

Cindy was a virgin and she was proud of it. She did touch herself once in a while and she liked the pleasure it gave her. She was fifteen years old when she had masturbated for the very first time. She had overheard a couple of the senior girls in school talk about that special spot between their legs. When she had gone to bed that night she tried to find it, and she did. It had been a scary but exciting moment in her life. A year went by before she did it again but as she grew up and began dating Tom, she began to pleasure herself more frequently.

A couple of weeks after she had met Klaus in the café, she had been to a birthday party and had a few drinks. When she came home, she had assumed she was alone in the apartment as Chantell had gone for yet another party. She had taken a shower and gotten ready for bed. She was in the kitchen drinking a glass of water when she saw Chantell's bedroom door open to her surprise.

"Can't sleep?"

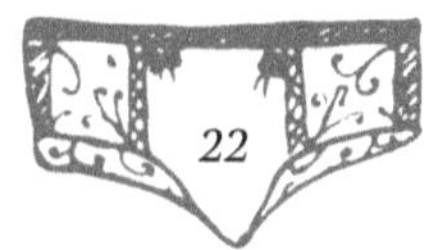

Instead of waiting for an answer, she turned around and found herself face to face with Klaus.

"What the hell? What are you doing here, Klaus?"

"Sorry, I didn't know you were here. Chantell told me you had gone out for the night."

Klaus was naked and Cindy's eyes were drawn to the long shaft hanging down between his balls. She closed her eyes and opened them again. She had seen Tom's dick once when she was younger and it was nothing like Klaus'. This was a man's cock and it was big.

"I ... I came home early," she stuttered.

Klaus came closer. Cindy only had a white thong and a thin T-shirt on. Her nipples were hard from the cold weather, and when he started to touch them, they got even harder. She knew this was wrong but the alcohol somehow numbed her ability to reason. When his fingers began to pinch and squeeze her nipples gently, she heard herself moan. Klaus cupped her boobs in his hands and slowly massaged them while looking her in the eyes.

"Do you like it?" he said.

Cindy was paralyzed. No one had ever touched her this way. She could feel his cock against her leg, and it was warm and hard. She put down the glass on the kitchen table with a shaking hand. She wanted this man, here and now, but she couldn't.

"I have a boyfriend."

"So? He is living far away."

"I love him."

Klaus kissed her on the cheek. "This is just for fun."

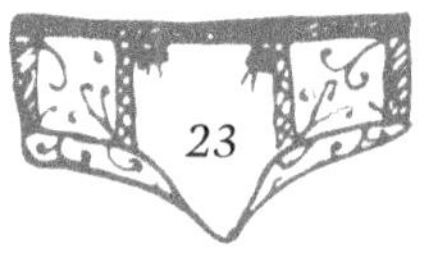

23

His hand took hers and guided it to his shaft. She couldn't help but notice that when her fingers were wrapped around it, the tips didn't meet due to its sheer thickness. Slowly he began to stroke himself using her hand. She looked down and saw a drop of pre-cum on the tip and she swallowed hard. This was wrong, but yet so exciting and the thrill of the forbidden was just too tempting. She closed her eyes and began to stroke him.

When he was close to coming, his moans increased. He took her head in his hands and lowered her towards his cock. She knew what he wanted, and she wanted it too. When her lips brushed against his moist cockhead, something snapped in her. She took him as deep as she could, and sucked, and licked like there was no tomorrow. She was only jolted back to reality when he groaned, "I want to fuck you."

As much as she wanted him inside her, she couldn't let him do that as she had to be Tom's virgin bride. She then turned her focus to making sure Klaus came. He was moaning even louder and his balls began to contract, she figured he was very close to coming so she pulled away and jerked him off with her hand. When he finally released his load, she felt the warm liquid on her throat and cheeks. Then it was over. Klaus took a few deep breaths and then kissed her on the forehead before returning to Chantell's bedroom. "Good night, sexy."

Cindy simply stood in the dark kitchen, shocked and ashamed at what had she had done. She went to the bathroom and took a long shower in an attempt to wash away the memories of what had taken place in the kitchen. When she was finally in her bed, she promised herself that Tom would never find out about what had happened that particular night.

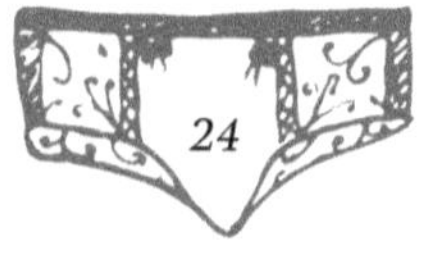

Chapter 4

Tom felt how his orgasm was creeping up on him but he was not ready to ejaculate. He gently pushed his wife's head away from his cock and she let go of it with a wet sound.

"Lie down, honey. I want to be inside you," he said.

Cindy moved onto the bed and put her head on the pillow while spreading her legs. Tom noticed that she was shaved, not completely though, she had left a tuft of hair just above her clit. It surprised him a little, but when he saw the wetness of her vagina between her swollen lips and the look in her eyes, he quickly forgot about it. He began to slowly caress her legs and inner thighs, moving his fingers up towards the prize. When his fingers touched her pussy, she was wet and hot, and she moaned silently as he began to rub a finger along her slit.

Tom was nervous; this was the moment he would find out if his wife had been faithful to him during the years that they had been apart. He moved up and she opened her legs wider to let him inside. His cockhead slid in an inch, and he felt her hymen. He smiled and closed his eyes, lowering his head so his mouth was by her ear.

"Are you ready, baby?"

"Yes, Tom. I am," she whispered back.

He began pressing himself inside her and she moaned a little when he broke through. It was like nothing he had ever felt before—warm, wet and tight. As he began to move deeper inside Cindy, she whimpered a little and then became quiet. After a while, he could only hear her breathing against his ear: warm and lovely. It made him even more horny. As he continued to thrust into her, she became wetter and she wrapped her legs around his waist to meet his every thrust. The muscles in her sex began to contract and at one point she became even tighter than when he had first entered her. It didn't matter that Mike had explained the feeling to him: there was no way anyone could explain the feeling of having one's cock inside a pussy in words.

Cindy had her eyes closed. She felt her husband sliding in and out of her, but that was all it was. She didn't feel what she had thought it would be like. It hadn't hurt much, just a sting and he was inside her. She opened her eyes and looked at his face. He met her gaze and smiled back, and then he closed them again. He lowered himself on top of her and hugged her close, while fucking her. She still didn't feel much, apart from his weight on top of her. She wrapped her legs around his waist, hoping that she would be able to enjoy the moment by changing the angle, but after a few seconds she realized it didn't help.

"Oh, I am close, honey, so close," Tom moaned.

"But I'm not ..." thought Cindy. Not wishing to upset Tom, she said, "Oh ... me too. You are so good, baby. Keep doing it just like that and I will come with you."

Tom felt his balls contract and his semen shot into his wife. Her legs pulled him closer to her body and she whimpered in his ear, "Oh, that was good, baby."

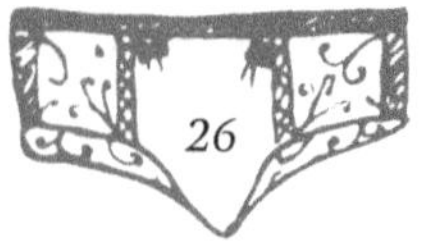

26

Tom was surprised at how tired he was. Maybe it was the wine he had earlier, or perhaps the incredible sex had really exhausted him. He rolled over and lay looking up at the ceiling. He decided to close his eyes for a second.

It wasn't long before Cindy heard him snore. She turned her head and looked at her husband. His mouth was agape and there was a dribble of saliva at the corner of his mouth. Her eyes moved down over his hairless chest and stopped at his limp cock. It was still wet from her juices and she lay there looking at it while feeling miserable and sorry for herself. Was this all she would get for the rest of her life? She got up and rummaged through her purse and found her cigarettes. She looked in the mini-bar and took out a miniature bottle of vodka. She then walked naked out onto the terrace and leaned against the railing. She would not have done any of these five years back: drinking, shaving her cunt and smoking were just one of the many things she had picked up from Chantell.

She balanced the little bottle of vodka on the railing and lit her cigarette. She took a long puff and slowly blew out the smoke, which lingered in the air on the windless night. The moonlight in the distance reflected on the ocean in front of her. She turned and looked back at her sleeping husband, and a tear formed in the corner of her eye. She wiped it away with the back of her hand and took another drag on the cigarette. Then she turned back to the ocean and drained half of the vodka in one gulp. She loved Tom with all her heart and she wanted them to be happy and have a great marriage together but after what had just happened, she realized their sex life was doomed.

Not only had he not touched her enough, he had no stamina. Maybe he would get better over time, she thought. Maybe she

27

could tell him that she wanted him to lick her pussy? But, how would he take it? He was Thai and his sense of being a real man was important to him. If she tried to tell him what she wanted, he might become angry and accuse her of saying that he didn't know how to please her. What would she say and how should she reply when he was right? That he had no idea what she wanted and how she wanted it? Then again, did she really know? After all, the only semi-sexual experience she had was with Klaus in a dark kitchen.

Unable to handle the questions bouncing around in her head, she finished the vodka, and opened another bottle. She stayed out on the terrace the entire night, drinking and smoking. She had not imagined her wedding night to end up like this. She had so very naively thought that she would have made love to her husband until the sun came out.

When Tom woke up the following morning, he found Cindy sleeping in the wicker chair on the balcony. He gently kissed her forehead and said, "Honey, what are you doing out here?"

She had heard him coming and had pretended to sleep. "Oh, I woke up early. It was too stuffy in the room so I came out here. How are you, my dear husband?"

Tom stretched his arms above his head, and twisted his upper body to flex his muscles. "I feel great. Wasn't it fantastic last night? I mean what we did? It was so beautiful making love to you."

She smiled at him, and said, "Yes, it was."

He looked down at his cock which was semi-erect. "Let's do it again, right now."

"No, baby. I'm a bit sore after last night, maybe tonight."

"Ah, so my big cock filled you up. I am such a stud."

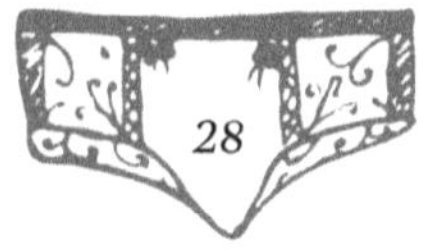

She watched the grin on his face, and said. "Yes, you are, my dear, and I want you again, but not now. Let's get dressed and go for breakfast."

When they walked into the restaurant, they found Tula and Ben sitting on the veranda outside. They made their way out, greeting the staff who came up to the couple to congratulate them.

"Good morning," said Tula.

"Hi, Mom. How are you?"

"Good, your dad and I had an early night. How about you?"

She nodded her head to demonstrate the same and so did Tom. A waitress came out and they asked for some coffee, tea and two bowls of fruit.

"When are you moving to the new house?" Tom asked Ben.

"Later in the afternoon. Tula wants to make sure she hasn't forgotten anything. She doesn't want to bother you during this period, and I want to make sure the hotel staff have done everything we've asked them to do," replied Ben.

"We have a few important things to finish up before we leave, so don't make any other plans this morning," said Tula.

Their breakfast arrived and they talked about the previous night's party. By the time they had finished, it was already ten in the morning and the tourists began showing up on the beach.

"We have expanded the hotel while both of you were away," said Tula, leading the way through the restaurant.

When they came out, she continued across a path and then onto the main road where she stopped. "Please, stand here, next to me."

Cindy and Tom did, and then Tula continued. "This is what the customers see when they arrive. What do you see?"

Cindy looked at the simple building made out of concrete and bamboo. The signed above it read "Hotel Paradise". There was a wooden gate at the entrance and there were bushes with violet and yellow flowers on either side. There was a flag post on either side one of the entrance, one with a Thai flag and the other with a Finnish flag. To the left was a parking space for five cars and to the right, another for ten motorcycles. There was a short path between the gate and the building and it was made of flat stones. The place was pristine and well maintained.

"It looks clean and inviting," she said.

"Exactly, and that's the way it should be. There is nothing worse than arriving to a hotel that no one takes care of. Let's continue."

They followed her and walked into the reception area. Behind a desk stood a man and a woman, both of whom Cindy and Tom had not met before. They were in their uniforms and wore big smiles on their faces, and congratulated the couple on their wedding. Cindy and Tom then walked out on to a path that took them through the ten bungalows that made up the hotel. All the bungalows had a small kitchen with a fridge and a microwave. There were no air conditioners and instead, there were big ceiling fans that ventilated the air in the living rooms and bedrooms. The path ended on the beach where twenty sun beds and parasols were lined up in two neat rows. To the right was a bar made from bamboo and hardwood. A young

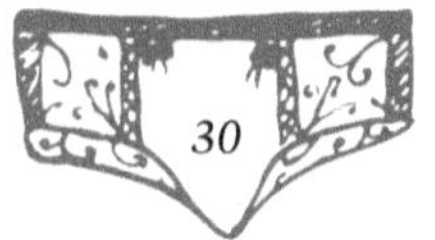

man was making a fruit cocktail for a female guest. Tula walked over and they stood in a semi-circle in front of the bar.

"All the drinks are made with fresh ingredients. The chef goes to the market every morning and picks up the fruit, veggies and other ingredients needed for the day. Even though each bungalow is equipped with its own kitchen, the majority of our guests prefer to either eat in our restaurant or dine outside the hotel."

"How many people work here?" asked Tom.

"Excluding Ben and I, we have twelve full-time staff and another four to help us out as and when necessary. All of them live around the area.

Just then, a man came walking across the beach and made his way up to the bar. He was wearing a pair of black Speedos and as he came closer, Cindy couldn't help noticing the bulge outlining his cock. She quickly looked away, but the sight of his manhood stayed in her mind.

"Good morning, Tula. This must be your lovely daughter and her husband," said the man.

"Hi, John. How are you?"

"Fine, the wife and I flew in last night. You were at the party so I didn't have a chance to say hi."

"Cindy, Tom, this is Mr. Helson. He comes here every year with his wife, and please remind me, Mr. Helson, is this your fourth consecutive year here?"

"Call me John, and yes, this is our fourth year here. We just love this place."

"Nice to meet you, John," said Cindy and shook his hand.

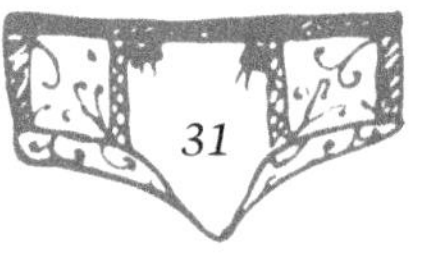

Tom did the same and then John turned to the bar and ordered two fruit smoothies to take back to his bungalow. Tula kept talking, but Cindy wasn't listening. She stood to the right of John and from there she could see his profile. He was in his late fifties, she figured, with a good body and with a lot of hair on his chest. Her eyes wandered down his body and stopped when they reached his cock. She wondered how big he was.

"Are you listening to your mother?" asked Tom as he nudged.

"What?"

"She is telling us how important it is to keep the kitchen and bar clean."

"Yeah, sorry."

Tom had seen her stare at another man's cock, and he didn't like it one bit. What was wrong with her? She was disrespecting him in front of her mother. Hasn't she had enough cock the previous night? He would have to talk to her about this when they were alone.

"Do you have any questions, honey?" asked Tula.

"No, Mom, I think we've got it. We can always pop by across the road and ask you if we have any issues."

"Sure, just remember to be on top of things. Make sure the staff put on clean uniforms when they are on duty and that they arrive on time."

As it was still early in the season and several of the bungalows stood empty, Tom and Cindy spent the rest of the morning talking to the employees and visiting the bungalows to speak to some of the guests.

In the afternoon, they helped Tula and Ben move some items to their new home, which was just across the road. It was

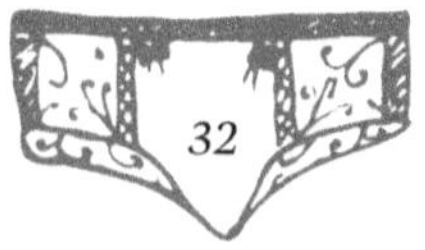

32

a beautiful villa and had a large terrace on the second floor from where they could see the ocean over the hotel. It had two bedrooms, a large kitchen, two bathrooms and a little garden in the back. Cindy was glad that her parents were finally able to retire and enjoy themselves after years of hard work.

On the way back to the hotel, Cindy took her husband's hand. "This is it, now it's up to us to run the hotel."

"Are you excited?"

"Yeah, and a little frightened. It's one thing to learn about hotel management from a book, but a totally different thing to be actually running one."

"We will be fine. Oh yes, before i forget, we have to go and see the lawyer and the banker tomorrow."

When the couple reached their bungalow, Tom pushed Cindy onto the bed and took off his clothes eagerly. Just as he was about to mount her missionary style, she put her hands up to his chest. "Hang on, I want you to warm me up."

"What?" Tom looked confused.

"Honey, sex is not about sticking your cock in my pussy and be done with it. I need some attention before that."

Tom began to blush and felt angry. Who was she to tell him what to do? She was his wife and should please him whenever he wanted. However, he managed to stop himself from lashing out at Cindy and instead, smiled at her and asked, "How did you know so much about sex?"

"I've been reading up on this on women's magazines and I am sure I would love it if you lick me."

"Oh, I don't know about that."

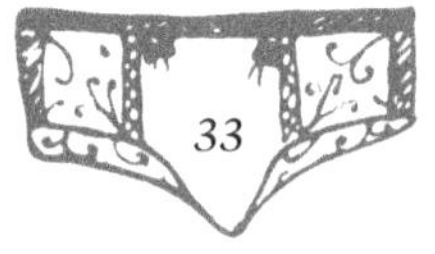

33

Cindy sat up in the bed. "Now you know. You liked it when I sucked you last night, and I think it's only fair if you do the same to me."

Tom thought about it. He knew many men liked licking pussy. Some of his friends at the university had told him stories about what they had done to the women they had picked up. Personally, he didn't like the thought of putting his mouth anywhere near her pee hole, but he figured that if he wanted Cindy to suck his cock in the future, he'd better do it.

"OK, baby. I'll do it."

Cindy giggled while she got out of her dress, panties and blouse. She threw her clothes on the floor and then lay down on the bed and spread her legs.

At first he wasn't really sure what to do, but he figured it was better she did not know he's new to pussy licking. He lay down between her legs and when his nose was above her cunt, he could smell her musky sex. He stuck out his tongue and tentatively licked at her outer lips. They tasted a little salty but it was not bad. She spread her legs a bit more and her hood became visible at the top of her cunt. He figured that it must be her clit and began to lick it.

"Oh yes! That's it. Keep doing that, honey," moaned Cindy.

He looked up at her as she closed her eyes slowly and moved her head from side to side. Her right hand was cupping her boobs at first and her fingers started to play with her nipples. She was becoming wetter, and now he could not only taste her slightly salty sex juice, but also something sweet and tangy at the same time. Her hips began to push up towards his face and she moaned louder.

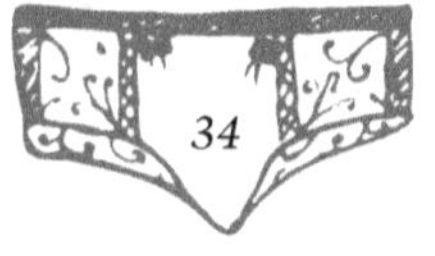

"Oh, darling, yes, yes! I can feel it coming!"

"This is fantastic," thought Tom. He had made her nice and horny, and almost ready to come using his tongue and now he could finish her off by fucking her. He then stopped licking and moved up on top of her and used his hand to guide his cock as he slid inside her.

Cindy almost shouted to him to continue licking, but it was too late. He was inside her and fucking her fast. His arms slid around her body and he hugged her tight while moaning in her ear. The pleasure she had felt earlier while he licked her had disappeared, and now she didn't feel anything else apart from his weight and that something was sliding in and out of her wet and unsatisfied cunt.

"Oh yes! Ah! I love you," groaned Tom, and his body trembled when he came inside her.

He continued to fuck Cindy even after coming and she decided to let him believe he had made her come too.

"Oh yes, baby, you are so good, so fucking good. Oh god, I am coming."

She hugged him and made some moaning and whimpering sounds and then relaxed. He rolled off her and lay on his back, gasping for breath. He then turned his head and kissed her on the nose. "Wow, that was just amazing! Both of us coming at the same time!"

"Yeah ... imagine that."

Tom got up and went into the bathroom. Cindy quickly slid two fingers in her pussy and let her thumb rest against her clit. She began to finger fuck herself, and within minutes she had her orgasm. She lay there with her eyes closed, enjoying the small

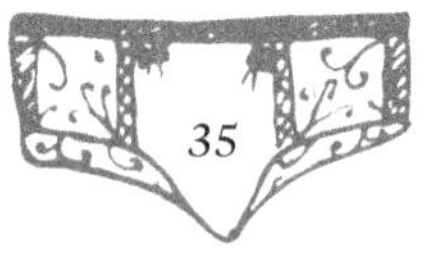

trembles running between her legs. Then reality hit her. She wasn't sure Tom would ever bring her to an orgasm with his cock.

When he came out from the bathroom, she slipped inside and locked the door behind her. She sat down on the floor and tears ran down her cheeks. She cried in silence and wondered what would happen to their sex life.

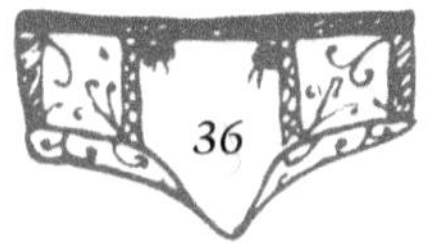

Chapter 5

he following morning after breakfast, Tom and Cindy decided to make a trip to the bank and the lawyer's office. The sun had yet to come over the hills so it was still cool. They walked along the dirt road for fifteen minutes until they reached the asphalted road leading them to the town. Along the way, there were farmers selling their fruits and vegetables to passing tourists and locals.

When they reached town, they stopped by a local mart for some refreshments. Cindy got a bottle of water and Tom had a soda. They stood leaning against the wooden wall of the small building, enjoying their drinks. Cindy lit a cigarette and slowly blew out the smoke. The nicotine rush hit her hard and her head felt light. She wanted to quit smoking but it was so bloody hard and she didn't have the self-control to do it.

"When are you going to quit smoking?" asked Tom.

She sighed and threw the cigarette butt on the ground, before stamping on it in resignation. "You are right, I should. I promise I'll do so by the end of the season."

He gave her a wistful look that indicated he didn't believe her.

"I promise."

"C'mon, let's go."

They decided to stop by the lawyer's office first. When they arrived, they had to wait in a crowded waiting room. The receptionist offered them tea and they sat under a slowly turning ceiling fan. Half an hour later, a short, thin man stepped out from the office.

"Ah, Cindy and Tom. It's been a while. Please come in."

"Thank you, Mr. Song," said Cindy as she led the way.

They made some small talk as Mr. Song took out a folder from a drawer and placed it on his desk. He then lit a cigarette and sat back in his chair. After taking a few drags, he said, "That's the documents that state that the both of you are legal owners of the hotel. Please read and then sign on the pages that I have indicated."

Cindy began reading and when she had finished the first page, she gave it to Tom. When the both of them had read the thirty-page document, Cindy said, "Everything seems to be in order."

"Great, now you can sign," smiled Mr. Song as he gave her a pen.

He then called in his secretary and asked her to make a copy of the papers. Cindy and Tom were quickly ushered out of the office, and left after getting their copy of the documents.

They didn't have to wait long at the bank and was led to the bank manager's office almost immediately. He was an overweight man in his late sixties, and in front of him lay two piles of documents.

"Good morning, Mr. Yun," said Cindy as she sat down in one of the two visitors chairs opposite the banker's desk. He grunted in

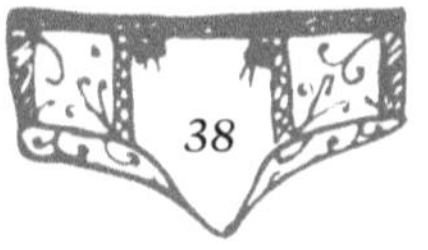

response and pushed one of the two piles of documents towards her. She picked it up and looked at the first page. It was a profit and loss report for the last three years.

"There must be something wrong," she said after she had read through it.

"Nothing is wrong. The hotel is losing money."

Tom frowned and leaned forward. "That is not possible. Tula and Ben told us the hotel is making a healthy profit."

The banker scratched his jaw and then pushed the second pile of documents towards them. "These will tell you why the hotel is in the red."

Tom reached for the documents, read the first page and looked at Cindy. "This is a mortgage."

"Actually three mortgages have been taken out on the hotel."

"How much is the total amount?" asked Cindy. She couldn't believe what she was hearing.

"Two hundred thousand ..."

"Bhat?" interrupted Tom.

"US dollars."

"But why?" said Cindy, her voice weak.

"Your parents have paid for your education and living expenses over the last five years. On top of this, they have also bought a yacht and made improvements to the hotel."

Tom flipped through all the documents before asking, "When is the next payment due, and how much is it?"

"Two hundred thousand dollars. You either have to pay up by the end of the month or the bank forecloses on the hotel."

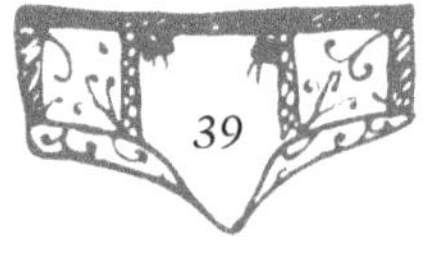

39

"That's in less than two weeks," said Cindy as she widened her eyes in disbelief.

"Yes, it is, and I am sorry. I would very much like to help you both but there is nothing I can do. We have strict instructions from the headquarters in Bangkok."

Cindy couldn't hold back her tears. "Oh god, what are we going to do? How could Mum and Dad do this to us?"

"I have no idea, honey. Let's go ask them."

They began the walk back slowly and by now, the sun was above the hills and burning into their backs. By the time they arrived outside Tula and Ben's new villa, their clothes were soaking wet. Cindy took a long deep breath and knocked on the door. She could hear someone shuffling inside and a minute later, Tula opened the door.

"Hi baby, how are you? You look terrible. Are you all right?"

"Mom, we came directly from the bank. We have been told by Mr. Yun that if we don't pay up the two hundred thousand by the end of this month, we will lose the hotel."

"I'm sorry, honey. We didn't mean to hide this from you, but listen, I am sure you and Tom can work it out. After all, you went to good schools, and I am sure our investments in your education will be put to good use. I am in the middle of a very important phone call right now and I will talk to you soon. Please take care and we love you."

Tula closed the door abruptly, leaving Cindy shocked and bewildered. "I don't believe this. What just happened?"

Tom looked as surprised as his wife, "Why would they do such a thing?"

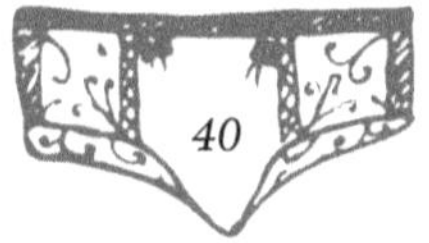

"Well … they don't care. You heard her. It is now up to you and me to fix this mess."

They made their way back to hotel in silence and it wasn't until they were on the restaurant's terrace that Tom suggested, "Maybe we can find an investor?"

"You mean sell the hotel?"

"No, we find someone who is willing to put in money for a percentage of the business."

Cindy looked at him. "That…would be like selling it. The amount owed to the bank would be the value of the business."

"You are right. What about renting it?"

"How do you mean?"

"I guess we can rent out the hotel, say, for two years and charge a hundred thousand per year. If we charge the money upfront then we can pay the bank."

"I don't think anyone would pay that kind of money."

They sat in silence and looked out over the ocean. A few guests were enjoying a stroll along the beach and two children were building a sandcastle. A hotel staff came by and asked the couple if they wanted something to drink, and they each ordered a jug of beer.

"Let's try the investor option. I hate to sell off the business, but that's the only feasible thing that comes to my mind for now," said Cindy.

"OK, I'll get on it. I know a few agency websites where we can post photos of the hotel and find out more information about potential arrangements that might work for us. I just hope some-one will contact us before the two weeks are up."

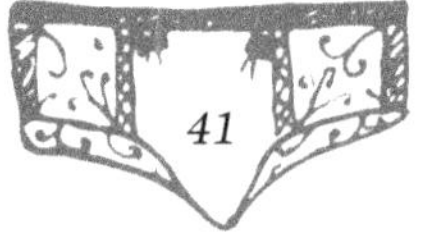

Back in their bungalow, Tom went online and began posting ads on the internet. He used photos from the hotel's official website and included as much details as he could. When he was done, he had posted on several different sites in Thailand, Europe and United States. He had even found a couple in Japan and Hong Kong.

He then sat back and thought about the mess they were in. This was definitely not what he had imagined life would be like after graduation. His parents had high expectations of him. They had invested their life savings in his education and now it looked like everything was going down the drain. He had hoped to be able to secure a comfortable lifestyle or perhaps, even an early retirement for Cindy and himself, but now it seemed that dream was evaporating with each passing day. With a huge sigh, he picked up his phone and called Mike.

"What's up?"

"Not much. We just found out that the bank will foreclose on the hotel at the end of the month if we don't come up with a huge sum of money."

"What?!"

Tom told his friend what the banker had said and when he was done, there was silence on the other end.

"Are you there, Mike?"

"Yeah, yeah, I was just thinking about something."

"What?"

"I know a guy who might be interested in investing in your hotel."

Tom's heart skipped a beat. "Who?"

"His name is Simon Taganaka—English mother, Japanese father. He lives and works in Hong Kong."

"How do you know him, and why would he be interested?"

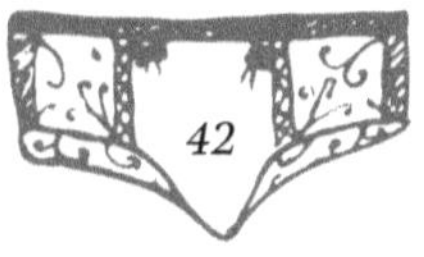

Mike chuckled. "He comes here once a year for a break from his wife and the kids. He hangs out at the strip joints and I supply him with some party favors."

"Drugs?"

"Oh, that's such a bad word. Just some weed once in a while. Anyway, last time he was here, he asked me if I knew anyone who was thinking about selling a bar or a strip club. At the time I didn't, but I think he might be interested in the hotel. I'll call him and ask."

"Thanks. I'll wait for your phone call."

As he put down the phone, the door opened and Cindy walked in. She gave him a kiss on the lips and sat down on his lap. "Who were you talking to?"

"That was Mike. Guess what? He might know a guy who might be interested in investing in our hotel."

"Really? I didn't know Mike hung around with people with that kind of money."

"Neither did I, but I guess he meets all sorts of people in the red-light district business. Anyway, he said he will call this guy and get back to us."

She kissed him again. "This is great."

Tom felt her perky boobs against his chest and his cock began to stir. He slipped the straps of her dress over her shoulders and kissed her soft skin around her round breasts. She giggled as he licked her nipples.

"Mm, that feels good, baby," she purred.

He lifted her off him and quickly took off his pants and shirt. He then pulled her close and she straddled his legs. His hands slid up between her thighs and reached her warm wet spot. "You are soaking wet," he whispered in her ear.

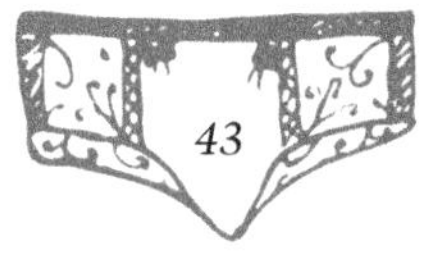

43

"Mm, I want you inside me, now."

He wanted nothing more than the warmth of his wife's soft flesh after what seemed like an impossibly long day and he could sense that Cindy wanted the same too. He quickly pushed her panty to the side and she adjusted herself so he could enter her. Then she began to ride him slowly while kissing him as his hands massaged her buttocks.

Cindy felt Tom's cock deep inside her. Although there was no real pleasure, that was the last of her concerns for now. She was glad he had thought about talking to Mike. Mike might not be a polished diamond, but he did know a lot of people.

Tom's orgasm was growing in his balls. He grabbed Cindy's hips and began meeting her movements. "Almost there, baby," he moaned.

She began making the right noises and squirmed as she felt him emptying himself inside her. She then pulled him close and said, "Oh baby, you fuck me so well." She then pretended to come and when Tom stopped thrusting, she climbed off him and went to the bathroom to clean herself up.

Tom sat in the chair with a grin on his face. He was so lucky to have a wife who came fast. He had heard horror stories about women who took hours to reach an orgasm and was very pleased that she came within minutes. On top of that, she was loud in the bedroom and he loved it. Her moans and groans totally turned him on.

Alone in the bathroom, Cindy leaned against the wall in the shower and rubbed her clit as fast as she could. The hot water helped her to relax and when the orgasm took over her, she closed her eyes as tears ran down her cheeks. "What a fucked up sex life I have," she thought.

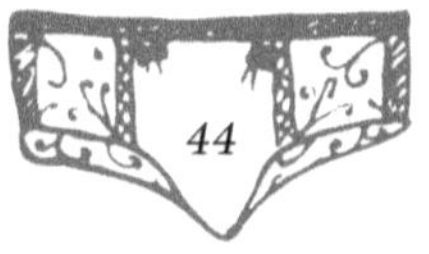

Chapter 6

Simon Takanaga looked out of the window. The day was cloudy and it had rained earlier. He drank some of his green tea and put the cup back on the table next to him. His phone rang and when he looked at the screen, he recognized that it was a Thai number.

"Yes?"

"Hi, it's Mike."

A smile grew on Simon's face. "Hi there, what can I do for you?"

Simon just turned thirty-five so he was only ten years older than Mike, but in terms of life experience, he was much more worldly and street-smart than the latter.

Simon's father had opened a sushi restaurant when he arrived in Hong Kong in the early 1970s. The business grew and when he met Martha Greensted, it was love at first sight. Martha had dated casually back home and the men she had been with were boring by her standards. An extremely attractive girl with honey blond hair and blue eyes, she had no problem finding suitors but no one was ever good enough.

Martha had stumbled upon the restaurant one rainy evening by chance. She had come to Hong Kong with some friends for a holiday, but had lost them in the crowd. The older Mr. Takanaga felt sorry for the young woman and offered to help her find her way back. She remembered the name of the hotel and when Mr. Takanaga called them, they sent a car for her. The next day, she came back and thanked him for his help. He offered her lunch and the rest was history.

When Simon was eighteen, the older Takanaga was killed while crossing a road in front of the restaurant. After the funeral, Martha and Simon decided to wind up the business and moved back to England. They ended up in London where she got a job with a cousin. Simon went to a college and it turned out he had a knack for languages. It wasn't before long that he was fluent in three other languages—Spanish, German and French, on top of English and Cantonese, and this made him a very sought-after relations manager. During his first stint with an electronics company based in Brighton, he was sent to Hong Kong to forge relations with companies that provided electronic components. It didn't take him long to realize that between Hong Kong and Taiwan, there was money to be made in contraband sales of electronics. Fast forward ten years later, he was married with children and had a net worth of ten million dollars.

"Do you remember asking me about bars for sale the last time you were in Ka Thai?"

"Yeah, sure I do."

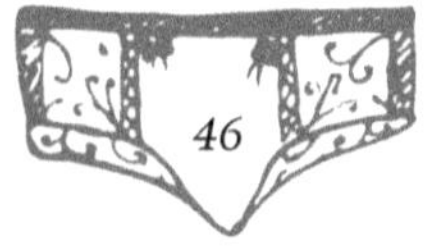

"Would a little hotel located on the beach be of interest to you?"

"How much and why are they selling?"

Mike then gave him a summary of the situation.

"It's kind of shitty to leave their kids like that," said Simon.

"I agree, but that's the way things are. So, are you interested?"

Simon thought for a minute. "Yeah, I am. You know what, I will be there tomorrow evening."

"Great, I will let them know."

When Simon hung up on his phone, he closed his eyes and groaned in pleasure. "Mm, that's it for today. You can clean yourself up and get me on the first flight to Phuket tomorrow."

"Yes, Mr. Takanaga," said the young women as she took his cock out from her mouth in relief.

Simon looked down at his dick and was glad to see that he was still hard. He loved his wife, but he was a man with an exceptional high need for sex.

When his secretary had left, he took a tissue from a box on the desk and wiped his cock clean off her saliva and his own cum. He then zipped up his pants and proceeded to make some business related calls.

Back at home, Simon kissed his kids good night and made love to his wife. He lay in bed listening to the sound of his wife breathing and thought about why he didn't feel bad every time he cheated on her. He had never been faithful to any of the women he had dated so it wasn't strange that he continued sleeping with others while being married. Even in his early teens, he had found women to be interesting and complex beings. While the fact that he had money later on in life certainly made things easier, he never had

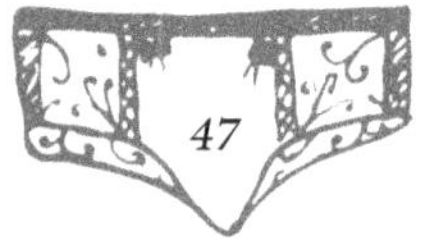

much of a problem hooking up with attractive ladies even when he was penniless and living in England. He would date a girl one evening and take her best friend out the next day, and they would fight over him even when he had made it clear that he was only interested in one-night stands.

His sexual appetite was only one of many reasons he liked to go to Ka Thai for long vacations. After all, it was the perfect getaway for some recreational drugs, plenty of pussy and a lot of drinking. When he had first met Mike in a random bar in Ka Thai, he found the young Thai annoying and even told him to quit following him around.

Then it had all changed on a particular night three years ago. He was back at his favourite strip bar and was enjoying a local beer when two white women walked in. They sat a few chairs away from him and he thought it was very strange seeing two foreign women in a sleazy bar. When the bartender brought him another beer, he started to make conversation with them. They turned out to be from the Netherlands and did not seem very interested in speaking to him. Getting the hint, he left them alone and turned his attention back to the bar girls who were now approaching him. It didn't take long for him to notice that the two Dutch women were slightly intoxicated, flirting with the waitresses and tipping the dancers. After a while, he got off his chair and walked over to where they were sitting.

"Hi, can I buy you ladies another drink?"

They both turned around and checked him out with their eyes running up and down his body. Finally, one of them said, "We are a couple and are not interested in men."

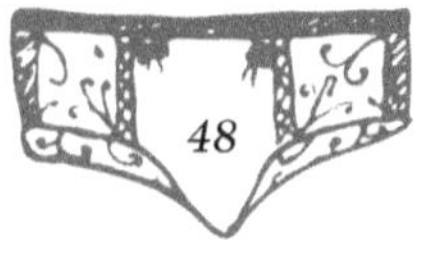

"That doesn't change anything. I would still like to buy you a drink. After all, it's not often that I see fellow women who appreciate the beauty of strip bars."

"C'mon, let him buy us a drink."

"Fine."

When the drinks arrived, Simon introduced himself and so did the Dutch couple. Their names were Hanna and Nicole. Hanna was a tall blonde dressed in a miniskirt and a sleeveless top. Her boobs were enormous and threatened to spill out every time she moved. Nicole was shorter and also blonde. She had beautiful green eyes and a smile that never seemed to leave her mouth.

As the night went on, the trio continued drinking and it seemed that the women genuinely enjoyed his companion. When the bar closed, they decided to go back to the girls' bungalow and continue the party.

It didn't take long before the girls were half naked. They were perched on a sofa making out, while Simon sat in a wicker chair opposite them. He had lit up a joint and was taking in the glorious sight in front of him when Hanna suddenly leaned forward and said, "Is it true that all Asian men have small cocks?"

Nicole's eyes were fixated on the slight bulge between Simon's legs and she started giggling. Simon then smiled coyly at them. "No, I guess some do, and some don't."

Hanna continued. "What about you?"

"Oh, I'm just a regular guy, I suppose."

Nicole managed to say, "Show us then," and began walking towards him.

"Well ... I thought you were lesbians?"

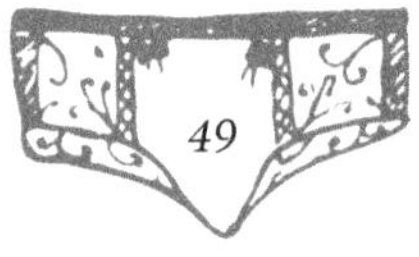

49

"So? We just want to know what we are missing out," Hanna said as she too, starting walking towards him in curiosity.

Simon took a long drag on his joint, and shrugged. "Sure."

He then got up, undid his belt and button and pulled down the zipper, letting his pants fell to the floor. When he dropped his boxers, both Hanna and Nicole's eyes widened at the sight of his crotch as they gasped.

"No fucking way," exclaimed Nicole.

"That's not real," murmured Hanna.

"Oh, it's real, I promise you that," grinned Simon.

The two girls looked at each other. Then Hanna said, "Go ahead, babe. Touch it."

"No, you do it."

They argued in Dutch for a minute, and then Hanna indicated to Simon to come closer. When he was standing in front of her, she slowly wrapped her fingers around his limp cock. "Oh my god, look, the tips of my fingers don't even meet."

While she was holding him, he began to get a hard-on and as his cock grew, her fingers moved further apart. "Jesus, I feel sorry for your girlfriends," said Nicole.

"Oh, I'm a gentle lover. Would you like to try?"

There was a sudden silence and it was completely quiet, apart from the sound of the night crickets and mosquitoes. Nicole then looked at Hanna, and said something in Dutch.

"So?" asked Simon slightly impatiently as he was getting horny.

Hanna nodded and answered Nicole in Dutch. She then turned to Simon. "She asked if it was OK. She is bisexual, and she wants to try it. I said it was fine."

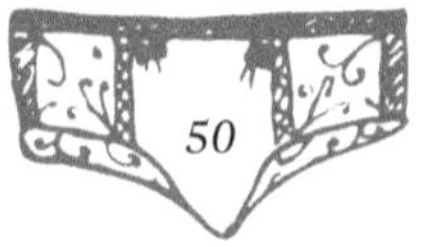

"That's very kind of you."

"I know she loves me and well … I don't have a cock like yours. As a matter of fact, I don't have a cock, period."

Simon laughed. "You are right about that."

Hanna then traded places with Nicole, who began to stroke his shaft slowly and then tentatively licked his cockhead. When she tried to take him in her mouth, her lips stretched so much that she closed her eyes and whimpered a little. Once he was inside, she slowly began to move her head up and down while massaging his balls. Sensing that it has been a long time since she had been with a man, Simon gently put his hands on her head and eased her into a rhythm. She didn't last long and came up gasping for air after just a few minutes.

"Oh my god! I have never even been close to anything of this size," she exclaimed while licking his shaft.

Hanna moved her hand onto her girlfriend's thigh and then inside her thong. She grinned and looked up at Simon. "She is wet and ready for you."

Simon pulled Nicole up and off the sofa and let her lie down on the floor as she pulled down her white thong. He then helped her with her top and bra. Her tits were small and firm but her nipples were hard and pointed right at him. He lay down between her legs and kissed each one in turn. Then he moved up so his cockhead was pressing against her wet swollen pussy lips.

"Promise to be gentle," she whispered. Her eyes told him she was a bit scared.

"I promise. Just relax and I'll do the work."

He began to press against her and when she opened up a little, he stopped and lay there. Then he felt her open up a bit more and

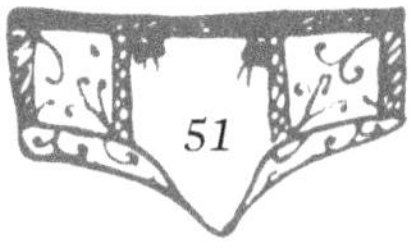

51

he pushed a bit harder. She gasped and he felt her nails on his back as she whimpered.

"Shh ... just relax, darling."

"How does it feel?" asked Hanna as she started fingering herself next to Nicole.

"Amazing, but it hurts."

Simon moved his cock in and out slowly and every time he did so, he slid deeper inside her. Then she suddenly opened up and he was all the way inside her.

"Oh, wow! This is out of this world," moaned Nicole.

"Do you like it?" he asked as he kissed her forehead.

"I love it. Keep going, I can take it."

He began to fuck her harder and after a while he changed position and put her legs over his shoulders. He felt his balls contract as the orgasm grew inside him. At the same time, Nicole began to thrash her head from side to side, and her nails dug further into his sides as she tried to pull him closer.

"Oh yes, yes, fuck me with your giant cock. Fuck me," she moaned.

When he was about to come, Simon pulled out and Nicole took him in her hand and he squirted all over her belly and tits. She then pulled him closer and licked the last few drops from his shaft and cockhead.

When they were done, they were both panting on the floor and Hanna went to get bottles of beer from the kitchen.

Simon must have fallen asleep after the marathon of sex, joints and beers. He woke up sitting on the floor, with a terrible headache. There was no sign of the girls. He then got up and went to the bathroom and took a cold shower. Back on the terrace, he got

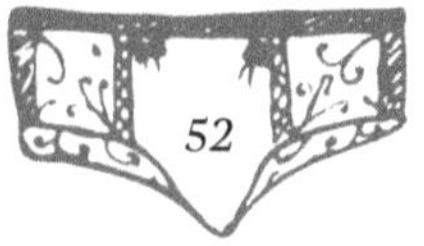

dressed and then looked around the bungalow. He opened the door to one of the bedrooms and found Hanna snoring on the bed. He looked down and saw Nicole sitting on the floor with her back slumped against the bed. There was a needle sticking out of her arm and vomit dripping down from her mouth. Simon rushed forward and placed his fingers on her neck. There was no pulse.

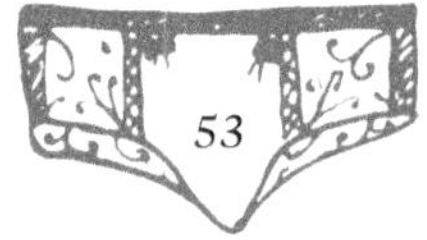

Chapter 7

Simon stumbled across the beach and frantically made his way back toward the hotel that was located in town. When they had arrived at the girls' bungalow earlier, there was no one at the reception and he didn't want to be seen leaving either. When he finally reached his hotel, the convenience store next door had just open for business and he walked in to buy a bottle of water. It was then that he realized he did not have his wallet with him. "Damn!" It must have fallen out from my trousers when I picked up my pants," he muttered.

He went back outside and sat down by the bench next to the hotel's entrance. There was a cool morning breeze coming in from the ocean and it helped clear his mind. The last thing he wanted to do was to go back to the bungalow, but he needed his wallet as his ID, credit cards and driver's license were all in there. Maybe he could pay someone to get it before Hanna woke up? He was still considering his options when he heard the sound of a moped approaching and as it passed him, he looked up. The driver met his gaze and stopped.

"Hey, Mr. Taganaki! What are you doing here?"

Simon realized it was Mike and decided to ask him for a favor.

"Hey, Mike. I just got back from a wild night. Listen, I forgot my wallet over at a girl's bungalow by the beach, and I am just too hungover to get it. Would you mind doing it for me? I'll pay you a hundred bucks."

Mike agreed without hesitation as he was broke and in need of some quick cash.

Simon gave him directions to the bungalow. Mike then turned his moped around and disappeared around a bend in the road. Shortly after Mike was gone, Simon realized he should have borrowed some money from him to get a bottle of water. He decided to take shelter in the hotel lobby and sat on one of the couches facing the entrance so he could keep a lookout for Mike. It wasn't long before Mike came in. Instead of passing Simon his wallet, Mike walked right up to him, grabbed his arm and led him to the restroom. He made sure they were alone before locking the door and turning around to speak to Simon in a harsh tone.

"Why didn't you tell me she was dead?"

"Sorry, it must have slipped my mind."

"Slipped your mind? A girl overdosed just a few meters away from you and you forgot to tell me about it? C'mon!"

"Did you get my wallet?"

Mike took it out of his shirt pocket and gave it to him. "I think this favor is worth more than a hundred bucks. What do you say?"

Simon pulled out three hundred US dollars from his wallet and gave it to Mike. "Here you go. Please forget what happened back in the bungalow and I promise that you will be my number one guy whenever I'm back in town."

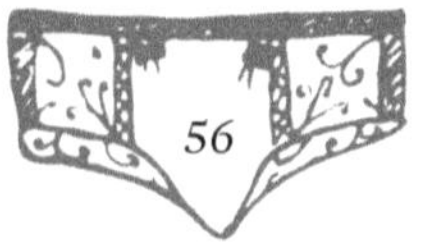

"Sure thing."

Simon then went back to his hotel and quickly packed up. When he was ready, he called the airline and requested to be put on the first available flight back to Hong Kong. Lady Luck was smiling on him and it turned out there was a red-eye flight that was leaving in the afternoon.

Simon only relaxed when he had crossed the Thai immigration borders and was on the aircraft. Thanks to Mike, no one would ever know he had been in the room with the two Dutch women.

The PA system jolted Simon out from his daydream and when he heard that the ferry had arrived at Ka Thai, he got out of his chair and picked up his suitcase. He was one of the last people to get on shore and he looked around for Mike, who had come to pick him up. He spotted Mike from afar and quickly noticed that there were two other people with him. One was a tall woman with piercing blue eyes and black hair. She wore a light yellow dress that ended halfway down her thighs and next to her, stood a man who was one head shorter than she was. He wore shorts, a T-shirt and flip flops. Mike waved to Simon and walked towards the trio.

Mike smiled and shook Simon's hand before making the introductions. "This is Cindy and her husband, Tom. They are the owners of the hotel that I mentioned over the phone."

Simon shook hands with Tom and bowed lightly to Cindy, as a form of respect.

"Nice to meet you."

"Thank you so much for coming on such short notice," said Cindy.

Cindy's voice was soft and deep for a woman. Simon liked her immediately and the fact that she wasn't wearing a bra under her dress made her even more attractive. A quick glance with his

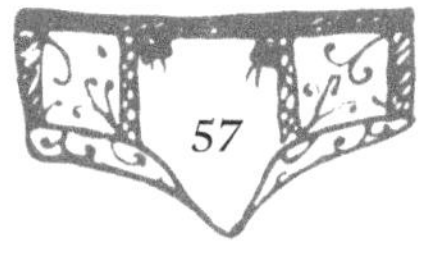

well-trained eyes was all he needed to know that her breasts were at least a C-cup. He smiled to himself as he had not expected to meet a woman like her—the way she dressed and the fact that she didn't wear a bra indicated she had spent a long time outside Thailand. What was even more interesting was that her husband allowed her to do so. Was he a submissive husband who let his wife make all the decisions? If so, it opened up all kinds of possibilities. Simon had no problem fucking another man's wife; he had done it before on several occasions, sometimes even while the cuckolded husbands were watching. It gave him great pleasure seeing other men staring at his cock while he plunged it into their wives.

"No problem, Cindy. I am always looking out for new investments and there is no better place than this paradise."

"Please come with us, Simon. We have parked our car a short distance away," said Tom as he led the way.

Back in the car, Tom and Mike took the front seats while Cindy and Simon sat at the back. Cindy stole a look at the stranger who was sitting next to her. He was tall for a Japanese man and she could clearly see the English blood in him. His face was longer and more oval than a native Japanese's, and his cheekbones weren't very high. His eyes were green instead of brown. After checking him out for a couple of minutes, she decided that he was a very good-looking man.

Simon turned to her and her ice-blue eyes bore into his. "How long have you lived here?" he asked.

"I came back from Switzerland a few days ago. I have lived there for the past five years, but I was born here on the island."

"Oh, did you study there?"

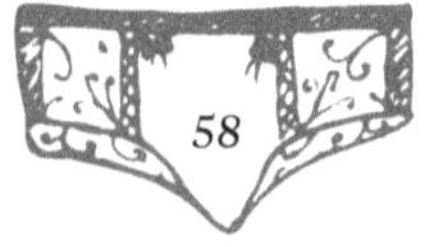

"That explains it," thought Simon. She must have picked up some aspects of Western culture while she was in Europe—one of them being not wearing a bra.

"Yeah, I majored in hotel management. Tom was studying in the States, in Kansas, while I was in Switzerland. We just got married."

"Congratulations! I wish the both of you a blissful marriage."

"And that explained, at least partly, why her husband allowed her to dress the way she did. Perhaps he was fond of the much more liberal Western culture? Or perhaps, he had even fucked one of those American cheerleaders?" Simon pondered.

"Thank you," said Tom "We will show you around the hotel first and we can have some drinks afterwards."

"Sounds good to me," said Simon and smiled at Cindy.

When they arrived at the hotel, Mike took Simon's bag and led the way inside. Cindy followed behind him and gave him a introduction of the hotel's history and its current operations. After checking Simon in, all four of them took a stroll along the beach. Cindy and Tom showed Simon around the hotel's premises while Mike stood on the terrace by the bar as he drank a beer. He was hoping that things would turn out well as Tom and Cindy had promised to give him some commission if the sale went through.

While he watched them, he couldn't help but think about how delicious Cindy looked. Her flawless skin had become darker over the last few days and when she walked, her boobs bounced under the dress like kittens fighting in a pillow case. He closed his eyes and fantasized about how it would feel like to have them

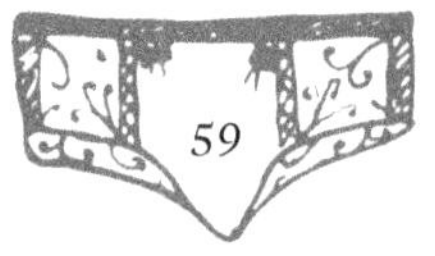

in his hands. Not that he would ever make a move on his friend's wife, but one could always have fantasies.

On the other hand, Tom watched how Simon had moved in closer to Cindy while they spoke. He put a hand on her shoulder and then the other on her arm. If he didn't know better, it would have looked like Simon was flirting with his wife. Tom closed his eyes and for a split second, he pictured the potential investor leaning in and kissing his beautiful wife on the mouth as she responded and they began to make out on the beach. He was brought back to reality and saw them walking towards him. Tom felt his cock press against his shorts and realized that the thought of his wife with another man had made him horny. At first he was confused as it did not make any sense to him. He then thought that his mind was playing tricks on him and making him suffer for letting Melanie suck him off that one time back in the States.

"This is a lovely place, Tom," said Simon as he put his arm around Tom's shoulder.

They then walked up to the bar to join Mike, who was waiting for them. Cindy ordered beer for everyone and they sat down at a table. The bar was relatively quiet except for a few tourists. After taking a few sips of his beer, Simon turned his attention to Cindy and Tom.

"Tell me. What does the bank want?"

Tom then explained what had happened and the bank's demands. When he was done, he sat back and took a long drink from his beer, watching Simon while he did.

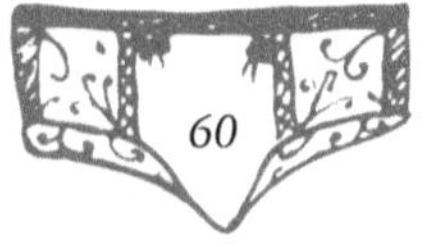

60

Cindy began to feel nervous and started biting her nails. This was the moment that they would find out whether it is still possible to salvage the hotel.

"We have a problem," said Simon as he looked at both of them intently.

"What?" asked Cindy, her voice barely a whisper.

"I can't own property in Thailand."

"I don't understand … what do you mean exactly?" asked Tom.

"The Thai law states that only nationals can own land and business, and foreigners can only invest in properties.'

"Oh," sighed Cindy.

There was an awkward silence as Simon emptied his glass of beer. He then cleared his throat and said, "I think we can make a deal, but what I am about to propose might not interest you."

Tom shot Cindy a glance as she smiled feebly back at him—there was still hope!

"What is it?" Tom asked eagerly.

"Well, don't take it the wrong way … but your wife, she is just too good to miss out on. I am willing to give you the money you need in return for a few days with Cindy."

There was complete silence around the table. Cindy looked helplessly at Tom, who glared at Simon.

"What do you mean?" demanded Cindy.

Simon then leaned forward, took one of her petite hands in his, and said, "I want to be with you. I mean sexually. I find you very attractive and you might say I have the hots for you."

"Do you mean that you want to fuck my wife?!" yelled Tom as he stood up from his chair and slammed his fists on the table.

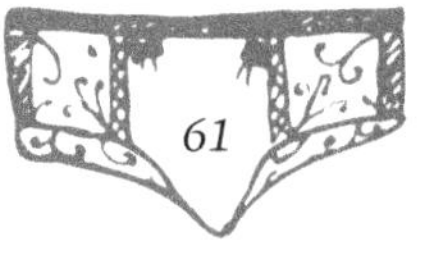

Part of him hated the idea of this stranger fucking his wife, but the other part of him was getting turned on by this unusual proposition. Tom swallowed hard and tried to keep his wits about him. He could not reveal that he was having split thoughts, and more importantly, she must never know about his rendezvous in Kansas.

"Yeah, that's exactly what I mean."

"No way! That's not going to happen. Thank you for coming, but you can fuck off and go back to Hong Kong now," Tom replied with a straight face before storming off. Mike quickly got up and followed him, while Cindy and Simon stayed behind. Simon's warm hands were still holding hers and even though his proposition was insane, there was something about him that attracted her.

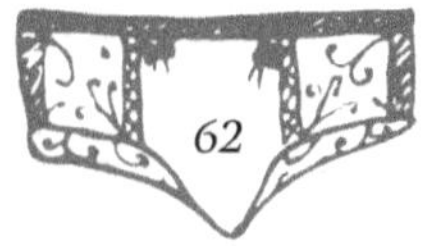

Chapter 8

ike caught up with Tom outside the hotel. He was sitting under a palm tree with his hands behind his head, looking up at the sky.

"I am so sorry. I had no idea he would propose something so absurd," said Mike as he leaned against the tree trunk.

At first Tom was silent. Then he started pacing around nervously. Mike was worried about his friend and put a hand on his shoulder. Tom suddenly flared up and turned towards him.

"You know what the worst part is?"

"No."

"I would let her do it. I would let that man fuck my wife to save the hotel."

"Why would you do that? Can't your parents help?"

"Ha! All their savings went into my education and they have nothing left. This hotel was my way to make sure they have a comfortable life, and now they will probably die poor and hungry on the streets."

"But surely, Cindy won't do it."

Deep down, Tom was hoping and praying she would. For some reason, he wanted to see another man fuck her; the thought was growing inside him and as it did, his cock became hard. He could never tell his friend what had happened with Melanie, and that he actually found the thought of watching another man having sex with Cindy extremely exciting. Thinking back, he realized that he had always enjoyed it when the other boys in the village looked at Cindy lustfully. He would even hide behind a tree and watch as they tried to flirt with her. Maybe as a teen, he had felt that he wasn't worthy of her and as an adult, he had unconsciously let Melanie suck his cock as a way to punish himself, knowing that Cindy would surely leave him if she found out about it.

Tom sat down again. "No, she won't and I am glad about that. But that doesn't change the fact that I can't take care of my parents."

"Let's go for a walk my friend. We can think this through," said Mike as he gave his friend an assuring pat on the shoulder.

Back at the bar, Cindy withdrew her hand from Simon's. "I don't know who you think you are, but I am not going to sleep with you. I love my husband, and I would never do something like that to him."

Simon smiled at her. "This has nothing to do with love, it is all about lust, and I am lusting for you. I have wanted you from the moment I saw you at the port this morning. I see nothing wrong with taking this opportunity to be together; after all you even might like it."

Cindy looked down at her hands in dismay. At first she was angry with Simon for even proposing such a thing. Then her mind drifted back to the last couple of days and the horrid sex she had with her husband. The guilt of what she was feeling overpowered her and she was about to start crying when a voice in the back of her head spoke to her—it was almost as

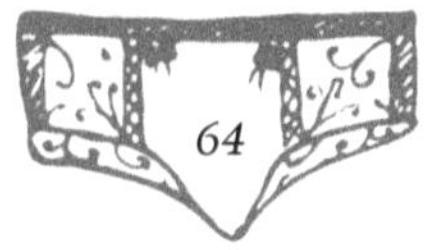

64

if Chantell was speaking to her and she suddenly remembered what Chantell told her over a year ago, "Cindy, sex is just sex. You don't have to love the man to do it. All you need is some kind of attraction."

Back then, Cindy thought her friend was simply a horny slut, but at this precise moment in time, she finally understood what she had meant. She felt attracted to Simon and her body wanted him. The issue right now wasn't her feelings, but rather how Tom will feel if he knew what she was really thinking.

She looked up from her hands and met Simon's gaze. He had a brief smile as he waited for her response.

"Simon, I don't know if I can do it."

She got up and walked down the steps to the beach. Her eyes were burning from the tears that threatened to explode from within. She had felt an attraction towards Simon while they were talking on the beach, and for a moment she had fantasized about being with him. Had he read something in her eyes that had made him think she wanted him? Was she that easy to read? Feeling frustrated, Cindy kicked a mound of sand and sat down by the shore in misery.

Simon watched her walk away and waved for the waitress for another beer. He had wanted Cindy ever since he had laid his eyes on her at the harbour. There was something in her eyes that told him she liked him too, but now it seemed he was mistaken. Not that it really mattered—there were plenty of attractive women in Ka Thai—but Cindy, she was something special. He waited for another thirty minutes and when it became clear that neither Cindy nor her husband was returning to the bar,

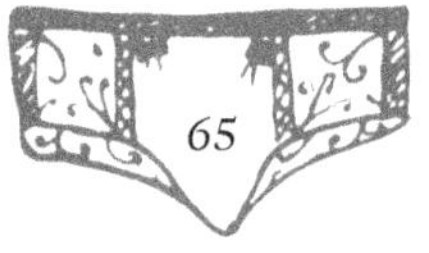

he walked back to his bungalow with plans for an evening swim and a light dinner.

Cindy was back in the bungalow and sitting on the bed when Tom walked in later that afternoon. She looked at him in silence as he took off his clothes and threw them on the floor. Then he walked naked into the bathroom and turned on the shower, his cock flaccid between his legs. Her mind went back to Simon. She wondered about the size of his cock and quickly closed her eyes in embarrassment. Just then, Tom came out with a towel around him.

"That's it then, we will lose the hotel," she sighed.

"I suppose so, if you don't want to sleep with that man."

His comment caught her off guard as she had expected him to make a scene. After all, most husbands would have done so if they had been presented the same offer. Instead, he sat down on the bed and put his hand on her leg.

"Honey, how badly do you want to keep the hotel?"

She was confused. He knew she love the hotel and would do almost anything to keep it.

"You know I want it, but I am not going to sleep with Simon to keep it. I don't love him. I love you, and you are more important to me than anything else."

"I'm glad you've told me this. But you know, I have actually thought about Simon's offer."

"What?" she pulled her leg away from him.

"Just listen to me. This place is all we have. It's for our children and grandchildren, and my parents' retirement. We will have nothing left if we lose the hotel."

"But ... we can always get jobs."

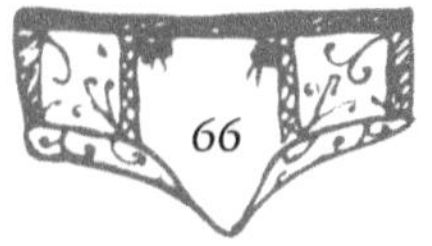

"Where? Not on this island and you know it."

She glared at him. "You are not suggesting I go to bed with Simon, are you?"

"I love you, and I know you love me too. We have our entire life in front of us, and a few days is nothing compared to what we will gain from this."

"You are insane."

"I'm not. All I am saying of you is to think about it."

She threw a pillow at him and screamed, "Get the fuck out of here! Leave me alone, you bastard!"

Tom had never seen her that furious and she had never sworn at him before. Knowing that there was no point trying to convince his wife, he went to look for Mike instead.

When Tom was gone, Cindy buried her head in the soft pillows. She cried like she had never cried before, and when there were no tears left, she got up and walked out to the terrace. The sun was setting and its rays reflected over the still water. A few tourists were still out on the beach and just then, she saw Simon coming out of the water. Even though he was a distance away, she saw his well-sculpted body–the result of many hours in the gym. He towelled himself dry and then walked barefoot back to his bungalow, unaware that she was watching him. Feeling frustrated, she went back inside and called for room service after taking a cold shower. She needed to clear her mind and think about how much she really wanted to keep the hotel and whether it was really worth sleeping with Simon. Perhaps she may have more to gain from this? Maybe what she needed was a good fuck? Tom hadn't been very good at that, but perhaps Simon was a better lover in bed? There was only one way to find out.

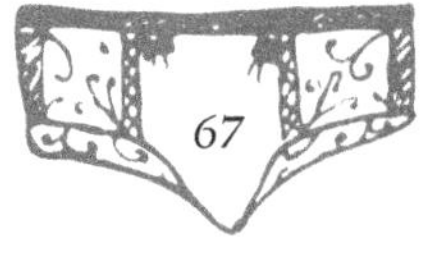

67

Chapter 9

indy found Tom and Mike in the beach bar, draining their beer.

"Tom, can I speak with you alone?" she asked.

Tom didn't answer. He simply stood up and followed her to the beach. The sun had set and a cool breeze came in over the water.

"What is it?"

She took his hands in hers and kissed him on the cheek. "I'm sorry about earlier. I have thought about what you said, and yes, I am willing to do anything to keep the hotel."

His eyes lit up and he hugged her close. "I know this is not the best solution, but it's the only one we have."

When he let go of her, she gave him a devilish grin. "There is just one thing."

"What?"

"I want you to be there."

"Where?"

"In the bedroom when I have sex with Simon."

Tom tried very hard to keep a straight face. He had been thinking about how he could get a peek at Cindy and Simon if she were to fuck him, and now she has actually invited him to watch them. Not wanting Cindy to know his true intentions, Tom pretended to look hurt.

She put her hands on his shoulders and hugged him from behind. "C'mon, that's the least you can do. I need you there. We don't know this man and for all we know, he could be a pervert."

"Honey, I can't even stand the thought of another man inside you. What do you think seeing the both of you together will do to me?"

"Please, Tom. I am the one getting fucked, not you," her voice slightly tensed.

He sighed and muttered, "Fine, I'll be there for you."

"Oh, I love you," she smiled as she turned him around and gave him a peck on the lips.

"Is everything all right?" asked Mike in concern when the couple made their way back to the bar and sat down at the table.

"Yeah, everything's good. Cindy has decided to go along with Simon's request." Tom muttered.

Mike guzzled the remaining contents of his bottle, took it from his mouth, and put it down on the table. Then he leaned towards Cindy with his eyes wide. "Are you crazy?"

She shrugged. "No, but we desperately need help and it's just sex after all."

"This is bullshit, guys. I don't like the sound of this at all. I love you both and I don't want this to cause a divorce."

Tom said, "Don't worry. I will be there to make sure nothing else happens between the two of them."

"And now you are telling me that you will be there to watch him fuck your wife? I can't think of anything worse than that and by the way, I am going to let you in on a little secret."

What?" Tom and Cindy asked in unison.

Mike whispered, "He has a monster cock."

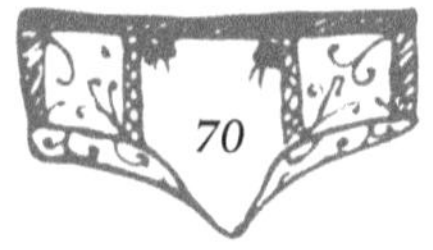

Cindy started chuckling so loudly that the guests seated at the next table turned around.

"How do you know that?"

"I know one of the girls he fucks on a regular basis whenever he is in town, and she told me."

"What do you mean by monster?" asked Tom, with concern in his voice. Even though watching his wife with another man was a huge turn-on, he didn't want her to get hurt in the process. Cindy might be tall but she had a tight little pussy.

"Well, the girl said it was like her forearm. Then again, she is really petite and could have been exaggerating."

Cindy pretended to look horrified when she was actually getting all intrigued. This might give her a chance to try something new. While Tom's dick was hard and thick, the thought of having a really big cock to play with did sound exciting. Realizing that both Simon and Mike were now looking at here, she responded, "Oh no, I hope he doesn't hurt me."

"Just tell him to be careful," said Tom before adding, "I'll talk to him."

Cindy asked the waitress for another round of drinks before asking Mike for a favor, "Could you please let him Simon know we would like to speak to him in person? He told me earlier that he would be leaving in the morning."

Cindy and Tom got up and left Mike by himself. After the couple had made their way back to their room, he sighed in frustration as he wondered what he has just gotten his mate into.

Cindy knocked on Simon's door.

"Come in."

When the couple walked into the room, the door, he was standing by the bed getting dressed.

"Hi, what can I do for you?" he asked while pulling a gray T-shirt over his head.

Tom answered, "Well, Simon, we have thought about your offer and ... we are OK with it."

Simon replied in disbelief. "Are you sure? I don't want this to be the cause for your separation."

"We are sure, but I want Tom to be around when we're doing it," said Cindy.

Simon grinned and then chuckled. He turned to Tom and said, "Oh wow, I had no idea you were into men. Is it mere curiosity or have you been with one before?"

Cindy saw her husband's face flushed and quickly defended him, "He's not gay or bisexual. I want him to be with me for moral support."

"Sorry, my bad. I just assumed your husband wanted to have some fun too. There is no problem if you change your mind. I have been some experience with men too, so it's cool."

"We are sure he is not interested. He is just there to watch," added Cindy as she glanced at Tom, who was looking extremely uncomfortable.

"Well, I have plans for dinner and I am going to check out a couple of bars later tonight. When do you want to do it?"

Cindy and Tom looked at each other for a moment. Tom then said, "How about tomorrow night?"

"That sounds fantastic. See you back here at ten tomorrow."

Simon walked past them and disappeared into the dark. Tom and Cindy stood in silence before Tom sighed, "OK, I guess that's it. Let's go back to our room. I need to sleep on this."

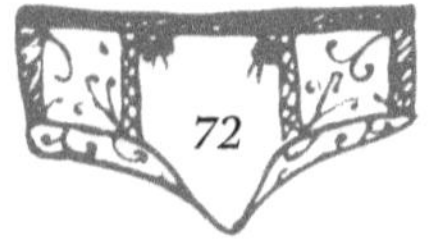

Chapter 10

Simon strolled past the hotel restaurant and through the lobby. Once outside, he lit a cigarette and looked at the dark sky. The stars were bright and the moon was rising over the hills. He took a deep drag and then slowly let the smoke out through his nose. He was pleasantly surprised that Cindy and her husband had agreed to his proposition and the look on Tom's face when he had asked if he wanted to join in the fun was priceless. The poor guy's jaw had dropped and his eyes were wide open.

Simon began his walk towards the town and made his way to his favourite restaurant. The waitresses greeted him by name and showed him to a table in a corner. Mike had already arrived and was studying the menu. He quickly put it down and waved out to Simon.

"They agreed to it," Simon said as he sat down.

"Seriously? I never thought they would do so," lied Mike.

"Well, you will be surprised at what people are willing to do when money is concerned."

"God, I wish I could fuck her."

"Why don't you?"

Mike ordered a steak and a bottle of wine for himself, while Simon pored over the menu. When the waitress left after taking their orders, Mike said, "I do want to fuck her, but I won't. My friendship with Tom is more important than that."

Simon shrugged his shoulders. "Your choice."

"When will you do it?"

"Tomorrow night. By the way, you should have seen the look on Tom's face when I asked if he wanted to join in."

"Why did you suggest that?"

"Cindy wants him there to make sure I behave." Simon grinned.

"Damn. That poor guy."

"Well ... I'm not so sure about that. I think Tom might have a secret."

Mike leaned in closer. "What do you mean? I have known him all my life."

"I think he is a cuckold."

"A what?"

Simon laughed. "Google it, my friend. Hah. A cuckold is a man who gets off while watching his wife having sex with another man."

"No way, Tom loves Cindy too much to allow that to happen."

"This has nothing to do with love. It's more of a fetish. He gets off seeing his woman being fucked by another man."

Taking a sip from his glass of wine, Mike slowly shook his head and muttered under his breath. "I don't see how Tom is a cuckold, but then again, what do I know?."

Simon said with a smirk on his face, "Exactly. And I am telling you, Tom definitely wants to watch."

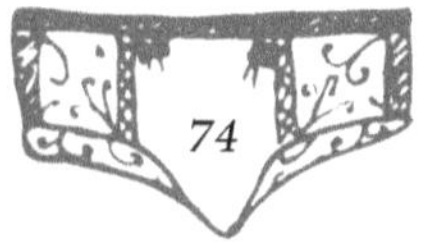

Their main course soon arrived and they talked about Simon's businesses over dinner. They continued the evening at a local titty bar and spent a few hours there before splitting up.

Later in the night, Cindy laid on the bed alone thinking about what she had agreed to and realized that she didn't feel guilty about it. It was nothing more than a simple fuck and Tom had agreed to it. It might even turn out to be a pleasant experience. After all, her husband hadn't been able to bring her to an orgasm and maybe Simon could do so. And if what Mike had told them earlier was true, at least he had a big cock she could play with.

"Honey, are you OK?" asked Tom when he came into the room.

"I am fine. It's just that I can't believe Simon would ask if you wanted to join us."

"Yeah, that was kind of odd."

"Maybe he finds you sexy," she giggled.

"It doesn't matter what he thinks. I'm not sucking cock and I am not letting him fuck me."

Just then, Cindy had a thought: she wanted to find out how far her husband was willing to go to keep the hotel.

"Just for argument's sake—what if Simon demands that you give him a blow job? Would you do it?"

Ignoring her question, Tom took off his clothes and headed to the bathroom for a shower. Before he closed the door, he turned around and said, "No, I wouldn't."

When he came out of the shower, Cindy pressed on the topic playfully. "What if he doesn't pay us if you don't do it?"

Tom was surprised by his wife's sudden interest in his willingness to suck another man's cock. "Why do you ask that question?"

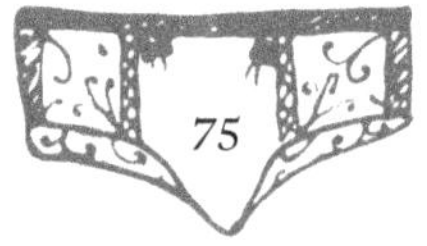

"Well, I was just curious. And like you've said, it's only about sex. What if he requests for it and I beg you to do it too?"

He sighed and lay down next to her. "I guess it would depend ..."

"On?"

"I don't know. I really need to sleep now. I love you."

Cindy kissed Tom's cheek and it wasn't before long that he was snoring. Lying next to him, she couldn't help but picture her husband sucking Simon's massive cock. For some reason, she found it to be incredibly exciting. She felt her pussy becoming wet, and slid her hand down over her belly and under her panties. She let out a quiet sigh when her finger tips grazed her warm and swollen lips. Her clit was hard and she began to rub it as quietly as possible while she covered her mouth with the other hand to muffle her moans so as not to wake Tom up. She whimpered and tensed her legs when she eventually came.

"What are you doing?" mumbled Tom as he stirred in his sleep.

"Nothing, honey, go back to sleep."

With a smile on her face, Cindy turned on her side and closed her eyes as she yawned. The last image she had in her mind was that of her husband's lips wrapped around Simon's cock.

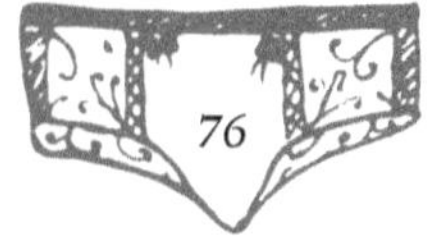

Chapter 11

he following evening soon arrived. Cindy and Tom made their way to Tom's room in complete silence as they held their hands. Tom knocked on Simon's door and he greeted them dressed in a pair of boxers and a white T-shirt.

"Welcome." he grinned.

"Hi," said Cindy uncomfortably.

"I have some chilled wine on the terrace. Would you like a glass or two?" asked Simon, after closing the door.

"That ... that ... would be nice. We are a bit ... nervous, as you might guess," stammered Tom.

"You guys just relax and make yourselves at home here."

The three of them sat down around a rattan table with a glass top. Simon poured Tom and Cindy a glass of wine each and then lit a cigarette. He watched the couple for a few minutes before finally asking, "Cindy, do you shave your pussy?"

The question came as a surprise and she replied shyly, "I ... I ... do, a little."

"What's a little?"

"I keep a tuft of hair."

"Well, I like my pussies shaved clean. Do you mind if I shave yours?"

Cindy shot Tom a glance hoping that he would intervene, but he simply shrugged his shoulders and looked at Tom.

"I guess that would be OK."

"Good, let's finish the wine and go to the bathroom. Tom, you can come too."

Feeling slightly flustered by Tom's unusual request, Cindy drank her wine as slowly as she could. She was extremely jittery and what had seemed like a good idea the night before didn't look so great now. But, there was no turning back and she knew it. She reluctantly finished the last of her wine and then stood up.

"All right, let's do it."

The guys got up and Simon led the way to the bathroom. When they were inside, he took out a razor from the cabinet and a can of shaving foam.

"Take off your clothes and get into the shower," he said to Cindy.

She turned around and removed her silk top and shorts. When she turned back to place her clothes next to the sink, Tom couldn't help but notice his wife's nipples were hard from the breeze coming in through the window even though she had attempted to cover her boobs with her bare hands. Simon on the other hand, had watched Cindy intently and he was very pleased with the sight before him. Her legs were long and shapely, and her ass was perfectly round. He only caught a glimpse of her boobs before she covered them, but they had been full and perky, with small chocolate coloured nipples.

"Don't be shy honey, there are no strangers here," he said.

He pointed to the bathtub and Cindy gingerly stepped into it. He then turned on the water and used the shower head to wet

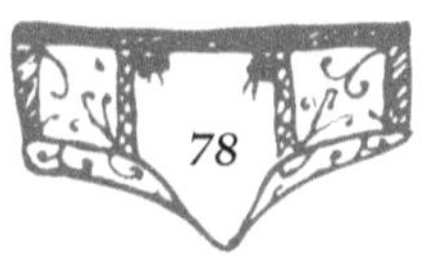

her pussy before gently covering it in foam. She sighed uncontrollably when he touched her and started shivering when his fingers came close to her clit. Tom gave her an assuring smile and she winked at him.

"Here we go, this won't take a minute," said Simon.

He carefully shaved her pussy and made sure it was smooth as silk. When he had washed off the foam, he took some lotion from a bottle and rubbed it into her skin. He smiled as he thought she had the cutest pussy he had seen in a long time. Her lips were swollen and her clit peeked out from its hiding place. He then helped her out of the bathtub, carried her to the bedroom and sat her down on the bed. It was then that he remembered Tom was still in the bathroom and as he turned around, he saw Tom standing uncomfortably by the door.

"Have a seat over there. It's fine if you want to come closer and have a look," he said to Tom and pointed at a chair in a corner.

Tom padded across the room. He pulled the chair near to the bed and adjusted it in an attempt to get the best view of the action, before sitting down. He looked at his wife and wondered how she felt. He was horny as fuck, but would never admit it. Earlier that morning, he had been hard and had jerked off in the bathroom before Cindy woke up. He felt guilty and excited at the same time.

Cindy watched as Simon knelt between her legs and then leaned forward. When his tongue touched her clit, she jerked back a little.

"Relax, you will enjoy this," said Simon.

He used his fingers to spread her pussy lips and then focused his attention on her clit, alternating between licking and sucking it. He loved the salty but sweet taste of her sex and when she began to moan, his cock grew hard in his boxers.

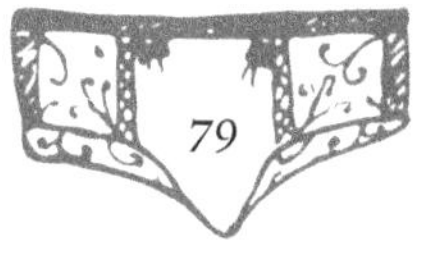

79

Tom leaned closer and watched intently as his wife began to push her hips against Simon's face. Her moans grew louder and her fingers dug into the mattress. "She never did that with me," he thought. Maybe he should have spent more time on oral sex. Suddenly Simon stood up and pulled down his boxers, and Tom gasped.

"That thing is … huge," he said.

Cindy lifted her head from the pillow and now looked worried, "No way, that won't get inside me."

"Don't worry. It will and you will love every inch of it," said Simon while slowly stroking his hard shaft.

Cindy couldn't help but kept staring at it. The cockhead was big and dark red. The veins along the shaft were on the verge of popping out and his balls were hairy and heavy with pre-cum. When Simon walked around the bed and stood next to Cindy's head, she instinctively knew what he wanted. She wrapped her fingers around his shaft and smiled when her fingertips didn't meet. Slowly she moved her hand up and down and felt how it grew harder with every touch.

Tom swallowed hard and when his wife opened her mouth as much as she could and took the cock between her lips, he sighed. He felt the pre-cum on his own penis and when Cindy began to bob her head up and down, it took all his will power not to pull out his own dick and stroke it.

After a while, Cindy's jaws began to ache from keeping her mouth wide open. She focused her attention on Simon's cockhead to give herself a break. She licked the tip and between his testicles and anus, and the taste of his pre-cum made her even hornier and she went back to sucking Simon's dick. She glanced over to where Tom was sitting, expecting him to look

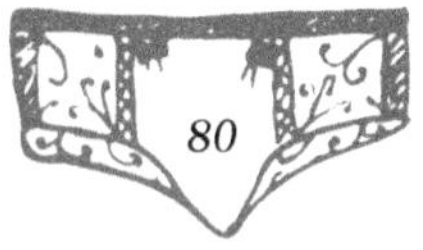

away, but instead he had a strange but familiar look on his face. It took her a second to register that her husband was horny. She tried to smile, but the enormous hard cock in her mouth prevented her from doing so.

Simon watched as Cindy began to slide her lips up and down his shaft. She wasn't the best cocksucker he's had, but she did a pretty good job. He noticed with pleasure that her right hand had moved down between her legs and her middle finger was rubbing her clit. He loved women who stimulated themselves and that got her some extra brownie points.

After what seemed like eternity, Cindy took his cock out from her mouth and gasped. "It's too big! My poor jaws need a break."

Simon smiled down at her and then turned her around so that she was lying across the bed. He stepped in between her legs and lifted them up. Then he aimed his cockhead against her swollen pussy and began to push himself inside her.

A flash of pain shot up her cunt when the first inches of his member entered her. Cindy bit her lip and closed her eyes. She tried to relax and breathe, but the massive cock slowly penetrating her was just too much to bear.

Tom didn't know what to do. One part of him wanted to get closer, but another was disgusted by what he was seeing. He could see Simon's shaft sliding deeper into his wife. Her lips were stretched as far as they could and then to his amazement, they opened even more and let another inch of Simon's cock inside. Cindy managed to take a deep breath and relaxed a little. Simon had stopped pushing himself inside her and stood still. Slowly, her pussy adjusted to the size of his cock and when she eventually opened her eyes, he was smiling down at her.

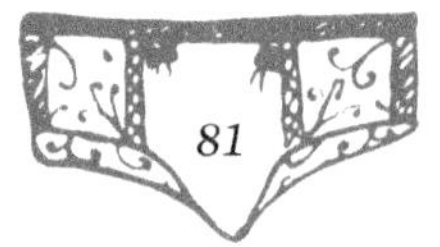

At this point, Tom's cock was harder than ever. He wanted to take it out to find release but he was too ashamed to do so. It wasn't the fact that there was another man in the room, but he had finally accepted the fact that watching Cindy with Simon made him horny.

"How does it feel?"

"I ... I ... it's amazing, but please take it easy."

He chuckled. "Of course, honey, I will be gentle. Check out your husband, he doesn't look too good."

Cindy saw what he meant. Tom sat on the edge of the bed, his face drawn and his eyes had a vacant look in them.

"What's wrong, baby?" she asked.

"Nothing, I am OK."

"He has just realized that he likes what he is seeing. I have seen that look before," said Simon.

She was shocked. Was Simon right? Was Tom turned on watching her being fucked by a stranger? The sight of her vulnerable husband sitting in the chair made her want him.

"Hey, Tom. Come over her and lick my pussy while Simon fucks me."

"Why? I am fine over here."

"Because if you don't, you are not the man I thought you were."

Tom was confused. How had a simple act of sex come to this—his wife threatening him? While he was reluctant to do so, he was somehow transfixed by the hardness in her voice. It was a command and it turned him on.

"I said, come here. Now," she called impatiently from the bed.

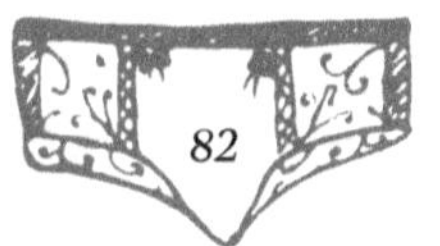

82

Slowly Tom got up and walked over to the bed. He looked down at his beautiful wife and then at the enormous cock inside her. He could only see the last few inches of Simon's shaft sticking out of her.

"Get on the bed and lie down, face up," she commanded, before adding, "Keep your pants on because you won't be using your dick.

Her words hurt him, but for some reason, it felt good being commanded by his wife. He did what she asked and when he was faced up on his back, he asked, "And now what?"

Cindy pushed Simon's cock out of her and then moved so that she was on top of Tom, her pussy hovered above his nose and her face close to his crotch, a classic sixty-nine position.

Simon understood what she wanted and slapped her ass gently. He then took hold of her ass cheeks and spread them so he could see her forbidden hole and her pink pussy below. He moved forward and when his cock was lined up with her wet lips, he pushed inside her with one thrust. This time he slid in like a hot knife through butter. He began to fuck her slowly, almost letting his cockhead slip out, but not quite.

"C'mon, lick my pussy," said Cindy in a husky voice.

Tom stuck out his tongue and let it flicker over her clit and as he did, she lowered herself a little and her pussy covered his mouth. Something was bumping into his head and it took him a while to realize it was Simon's balls smacking him with every thrust. This was humiliating and exciting at the same time. As Tom began to unzip his pants, Cindy said, "Don't. You are not allowed to jerk off. Just eat my pussy and be a good boy."

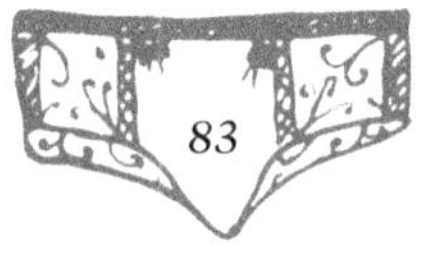

Simon couldn't hold back much longer. He grabbed on to Cindy's soft hips and began to slam into her, harder and faster with every thrust. She lifted her head up and looked at him over her shoulder.

"Oh yeah, fuck my pussy. Fuck it hard."

Cindy felt a warm feeling grew from inside that radiated throughout her body. It was as if little electric currents were flowing through her nerves and then suddenly, all the currents converged at one spot and she exploded in her first cock-made orgasm. She moaned, whimpered, and finally screamed in ecstasy. When the last wave of pleasure had passed, she lied down on her husband, with Simon's cock still inside her. Simon continued to fuck her before pulling out his cock, with his cum raining down on her lower back and ass in hot droplets.

By this time, Tom could hardly breathe and his face was wet from Cindy's juices. He pushed his wife to the side and gasped for air. He then swung his legs over the bed and walked straight into the bathroom. The first thing he did was to jerk off and when he had come, he washed his face and took off his shirt.

Simon looked down at the beautiful woman lying on her stomach in front of him. She breathed heavily. Sensing that Simon was looking at her, she rolled over and looked up at him.

"Thank you," she said.

"You are welcome."

"That was the first time I have had an orgasm with a man."

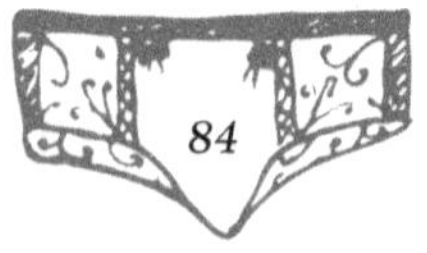

Simon's cock was still hard and she sat up and reached for it. She licked the cockhead and then slowly began to stroke him.

"I think you'd better go," he said.

"Why?"

"Tom probably won't like staying here when he comes out."

She kissed his cock one last time. "Yeah, you are right."

"So, shall we say the same time tomorrow?"

She smiled up at him as she got dressed. "Yes, that sounds nice."

Simon waited by the bathroom door and when Tom came out, they nodded to each other. Tom then took Cindy's hand and they left.

When they got back to their bungalow, Tom sat down at the dinner table and looked furious.

"Listen, honey and before you say anything, let me explain what I felt," she said.

Tom didn't answer. Instead he poured himself some wine and started fidgeting with the wine glass.

"What do you have to say?" he asked while twisting the stem of the glass.

Cindy sat down in the chair opposite him.

"The truth is, you have never made me come. I have always faked it. I am sorry, I should have told you. I do love you with all my heart, but what happened earlier tonight was the first time I have ever done anything like this. It felt good when you ate my pussy while Simon fucked me. I am sorry if I sound like a bitch, but that's what I felt."

Tom put his face in his hands and confessed, "Baby, I must tell you that even though I felt humiliated by what happened, I did enjoy being commanded by you."

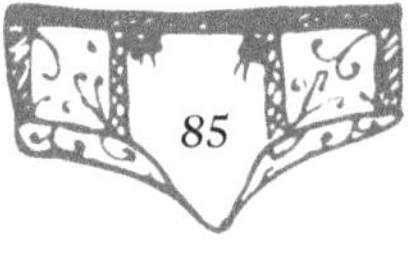

"Really?!"

"Yeah," he laughed.

Cindy got up and made her way to where he was sitting. She went down on her knees and took his face in her hands. She kissed him and when their lips finally parted, she said, "I love you and and thank you for letting me do this."

"Let's go to bed. You will need all the rest you can get before tomorrow night."

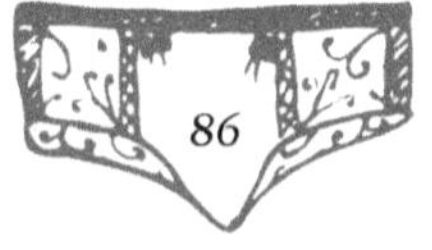

Chapter 12

The following day, Cindy and Tom pretended that nothing was amiss and made their way around the hotel. They could not even show the slightest sign that there were financial problems or the staff might quit.

The hotel was almost full and the majority of the customers were Europeans who were escaping the cold weather up north. Their skin shone in the sun and in a few days it would turn pink. When their vacation was coming to an end, they would finally a shade of golden brown. Cindy thought it was strange watching them lying like sausages on the beach as they turn over every so often to get an even tan.

The couple walked along the beach and Tom pointed out that some of the sunbeds and parasols had to be changed. They were rusted and looking bad, and could pose a danger to the tourists. Cindy made a mental note as the couple continued walking hand in hand.

Simon sat on his terrace and watched them. He thought that they made a cute couple. He honestly hoped that they would eventually make it as hotel owners with his help. He couldn't help but thought about the previous night and grinned as he stretched his arms above his heads as he twisted his back a little.

There were a few pops and his spine clicked into place. Cindy had turned out to be a lot hotter than he had thought. He had been sure she would lie on the bed and let him fuck her and little else. To his surprise she had been quite active and even had Tom join them. He thought it was fascinating that he had actually done what she asked. Many other husbands would have told their wife to fuck off at that point. What did that say about the man? He might be completely pussy-whipped, but Simon didn't think so. He thought that Tom actually got turned on by watching his wife being fucked by another man, and that was something that Simon could understand.

Before being married to his present wife, he had been living with an American woman for a few years and she was into swinging. It was a lot of fun at the beginning but things soon turned sour when she realized that he got more pussy than she had cock. By then, he was enjoying too much of the lifestyle to give it up and the couple went their separate ways when she wanted out. Simon wondered if Tom liked being cuckolded. Either that or he might be insecure, or couldn't please Cindy in bed and when he had seen and heard her come, it had turned him on. He made a mental note to step it up this evening and see how far Tom was willing to go.

When the couple had disappeared from his view, Simon stood up and went inside his room. He needed to make some business calls and take a shower. He had decided to go sightseeing in the morning and get a tan by the beach in the afternoon. He loved going up into the hills on a Vespa to enjoy the fresh cool air and the scenic view.

Stopping and turning her head back to adjust her sandals, Cindy had seen Simon watching them and had wondered what

was going through his mind. Had he enjoyed being with her? Was it what he had expected? He had looked a bit surprised the night before when she had told Tom to lick her pussy while he fucked her, and she must confess that she had enjoyed that, almost as much as humiliating Tom. She didn't mean to make her husband uncomfortable, but watching him lick her pussy while he was getting slammed in the head by Simon's balls had been a huge turn-on for her. The thought of it made her blush.

"What is it, baby?" asked Tom

"Oh, nothing special."

Cindy wondered if she could get her husband to suck Simon's cock. That would be an amazing sight. She then shook her head to get rid of the perverted thoughts and took Tom's hand. They began to run along the beach and as she pulled him with her to the left, they stumbled into the water. They both fell over after a few steps and when the both of them got up, they were sputtering seawater.

"What the hell did you do that for?" asked Tom as he chuckled.

Cindy laughed. "Do you remember how we used to do this all the time?"

"Yeah, but we were kids then."

"So? We can still have fun, can't we?"

Tom took out his wet mobile phone from his back pocket. "Yeah, but it cost me a new phone."

"Oh baby, I'm so sorry. Let's get changed and go to town. I'll buy you a new one."

Tom kissed her and when her boobs pressed against his chest, his cock rose to attention as he felt her hard nipples through her

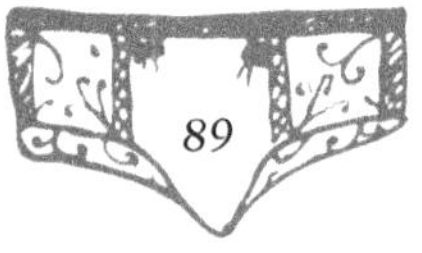

wet blouse. His thin shorts didn't conceal the bulge and Cindy began stroking his back gently.

"I see, you want some of me right now?" she purred in his ear.

"Yeah, that would be nice."

She kissed him on the cheek. "Let's save it for tonight."

Tom was confused. "What about Simon?"

She gave him a wicked grin. "Exactly, let's save it for Simon."

"But ..."

She took off running and Tom watched her for a minute before setting off after her. His wife was changing and he didn't know if he liked it or not.

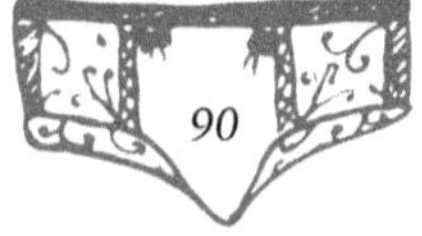

Chapter 13

Simon was enjoying a whiskey over ice when he heard a knock on the door. He opened the door and was surprised to see the young couple standing outside.

"You are early," he said.

Cindy smiled at him. "Yeah, we are. We have just been invited to some friends' place for a party. I'm sorry for not telling you in advance."

She was dressed in a white thin dress and when he stepped aside to let them in, he noticed that she didn't wear a bra. Her boobs bounced seductively under the thin fabric. He wondered if she was wearing any panties, but he would soon find out.

Tom followed behind. He shook hands with Simon and pointed at his glass. "Can I have one?"

"Of course. Would you like a drink, Cindy?"

She turned around and replied, "No, I am fine."

When they were seated on the terrace, Cindy said, "What did you do today apart from watching me and Tom walk along the beach?"

Simon laughed. "You saw me?"

"Yeah, I did."

Simon drank more of his whiskey and lit a cigarette. "I went up into the hills for a few hours. I wanted to go to the beach in the afternoon, but a few business calls came in so I ended up here instead."

The sound of music and laughter drifted in the air. Somewhere a baby was crying and in the midst of these, there was the sound of crickets chirping in the distance. They sat in silence for a while taking in the mishmash of symphony when Cindy suddenly asked, "Are you married, Simon?"

"Yes, I am."

"Really? I thought you were single," Tom blurted out in surprise.

"I have been married for five years."

"Is she Japanese?"

"No, she is Chinese. I met her in Hong Kong during a business trip and one thing quickly led to another."

"Do you love her?" asked Cindy.

"Of course I do."

Tom reached for his glass and after taking a long sip, he asked, "Why then do you sleep with other women? I guess Cindy isn't your first."

Simon chuckled. "You are right, she isn't. I don't know why I do it. I guess it's because I find women fascinating and I can't keep my hands off them."

"What will happen if your wife finds out?" pressed Cindy.

"Oh, I suppose she knows even though she has never said anything about it. I am very discreet but she must have suspected it for a while now."

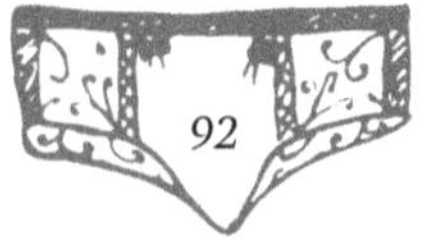

"Do you do sleep with other women back in Hong Kong or do you do so only when you travel?" said Tom.

"I never do it at home. I prefer to play around in different countries. Maybe I am just curious about pussies from different parts of the world."

Cindy laughed. "With me, you got a two for one."

"How do you mean?"

"My dad is Thai but my mother is Finnish."

"That explains those beautiful eyes you have."

She blushed. "Thanks."

Simon finished his drink and asked if they wanted anything else. Cindy and Tom shook their heads and Simon smiled, "Let's have some fun then. We have a lot to do before you meet your friends."

Cindy was already wet. When she followed Simon into the bedroom, she almost moaned out loud just thinking about his cock sliding in and out of her. She glanced back at Tom who was a few steps behind her. He looked serious and she gave him a wink. He smiled back and patted her ass. When the door closed behind them, Cindy felt an almost immediate change within herself. Her desire for Simon and her loathing of her husband's inability to make her come came out in the form of a demand.

"Tom, undress Simon and take out his cock," she instructed.

Tom was stunned for a moment as he tried to register what Cindy had just said. He muttered confusedly, "What?"

"You heard me. Take off his clothes."

He looked at her in her eyes and was instantly reminded of a tiger looking at its prey as she stood opposite him with her hands akimbo. There was a fierce hunger he had never seen before and

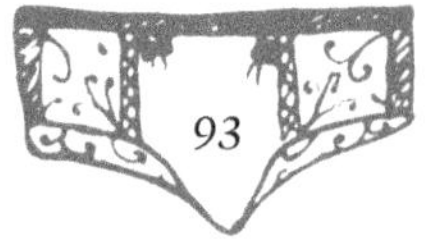

he wondered what happened to the placid, good-humoured and wonderful woman he has known all these years. What he was seeing now brought him back to the time he was with Melanie. With a sigh, he decided to go along with what Cindy requested, mostly because he felt guilty about what he had done with Melanie, even though he must admit it was a turn-on for him.

Simon stood still in silent amusement while Tom helped him off with his shirt and then unzipped his pants. When they fell to the floor, Simon stepped out of them. Tom turned to Cindy, half expecting her to apologize for what she had just asked him to do.

"The boxers too," she demanded.

Standing in front of Simon, he pulled down at the hems of his boxers and when Simon's cock sprung out, he took a step back.

"OK, here it is. All done," he said.

Cindy came over to the bed and sat down on the edge. She took Simon's hand and pulled him closer so he was standing between her legs. His hard cock was only inches from her face.

"Tom, feed me his cock," she said.

With a trembling hand, Tom took Simon's shaft and steered it towards Cindy's open lips. She stuck out her tongue and let it run over and around the swollen cockhead. Tom let go when her lips slid over it and stepped back. She then grabbed his hand and mumbled, "Don't go anywhere. I want you to watch me suck his cock."

Meanwhile, Simon closed his eyes and enjoyed her warm lips around him. He thought it was interesting how she had made her husband help her suck another man's cock and how Tom had played along. That was something that earned his respect.

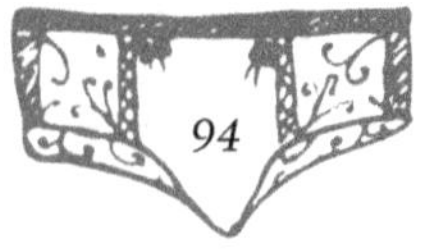

As Tom's cock slid in and out of Cindy's wide open mouth, she began to play with her pussy. She didn't wear any underwear and she was so wet that Simon could hear the sound of her fingers sliding in and out of her. She watched her husband standing next to her and his eyes were fixed on her mouth. He swallowed hard and then gave her a smile.

Tom had a hard-on like never before. Watching how Simon's cock slid in and out of his wife made him almost come. He could smell her juices now and he wanted to be part of the game. He pulled down his zipper and was about to take out his cock when Cindy stopped him.

"No, no, you don't get to play. You just watch and learn."

"But ..."

"Oh! Shut up and sit down next to me."

He did as he was told and she continued to suck and lick Simon's cockhead. She took his balls in her free hand and slowly massaged them. She then used her other hand to finger fuck her hot and by now, very wet pussy.

Simon was close to coming and wanted to bury his cock in Cindy's cunt. He stepped back and his cock slid out of her mouth with a wet plop.

"Why?" she begged.

"Give me your ass. I want to fuck you from behind," he said in a husky voice.

Cindy did what he wanted and pushed her ass towards him before grinning and saying to Tom. "I want you to lick my ass."

Tom nodded dumbly as he repositioned himself. His tongue began to flicker over her tight hole and she started moaning. The moans became whimpers as Simon pushed himself

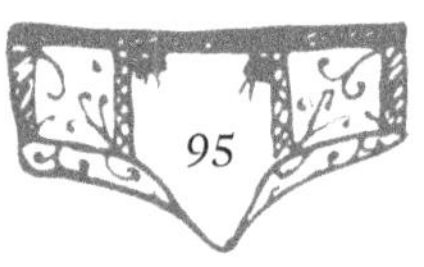

into her pussy, and she started screaming when he began to fuck her.

The sensation of her husband's tongue and the big cock inside her made Cindy want to cry in pleasure. She had never thought sex could be so delicious and exciting at the same time. That one night in the kitchen in her apartment was nothing compared to this. She only wished that Tom could make her feel this way. As Simon began to fuck her harder, she wanted to punish her husband even more. She turned her head and looked at the two men over her shoulder.

"I want you to suck him, Tom."

Her husband looked at her and shook his head. "No, I won't."

"You will if you want to sleep in my bed tonight."

Simon was so horny by now that the only thing he wanted to do was to come and he didn't care if it was Cindy's beautiful pussy or Tom's lips that made him do so.

"C'mon Tom, be a sport. It doesn't make you gay. Look at it as a way of pleasing your beautiful wife. You want her to be happy, don't you?"

"I ... I ... do," Tom stammered.

He felt Cindy moved and then suddenly she was sitting next to him. She had one arm around his shoulder and her fingers were wrapped around Simon's cock. Tom watched as the cock came closer to his face and when it was just an inch away, he could smell his wife's juices on it, she whispered, "Open your mouth and close your eyes, honey."

He did it and then he felt the softest thing against his lips. It was warm and felt like silk. He didn't dare to open his eyes. His lips spread wider as his wife slowly pushed Simon's cock inside.

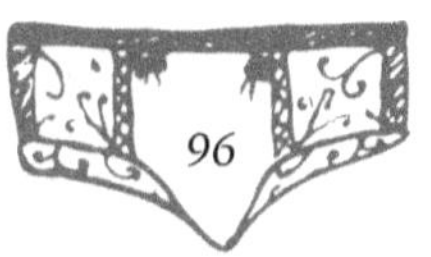

When it touched the back of his throat, she whispered, "Good. Now move your head up and down."

Cindy almost came right then and there when she saw Tom with his mouth wide open and when he began bobbing his head up and down, she moaned aloud. "Just like that, honey. What you are doing is simply beautiful," she whispered in his ear. Her hand slid down to his cock and he was hard.

Tom felt her hands stroking his cock and sighed with pleasure. At least she would jerk him off and that made sucking Simon almost worthwhile.

Simon was enjoying the moment but he didn't want to come in Tom's mouth. He slowly pushed Tom's face away when he felt his orgasm approaching. Seeing that, Cindy immediately stopped fondling Tom's cock and took Simon's member in her mouth instead.

"What? Why did you stop?" groaned Tom.

Cindy didn't answer and instead, she focused on sucking Simon's harder. Within a few seconds, Tom heard Simon moan and saw his wife swallowing his juices.

Simon looked down and was impressed. She hadn't spilled a drop. She had even licked his cockhead and make sure that it was clean before turning to her husband.

"Now, you can jerk off over there in the corner."

"Why can't you do it?"

She sighed. "Because you don't deserve it yet."

Tom got up and walked over to where she had pointed. His cock was still hard and when he began to stroke himself, he heard his wife pleading, "C'mon Simon, fuck me. I want to come."

She moved up on the bed and lay down on her back. Simon pushed a pillow under the small of her back and hips to bring her pussy off the sheets. When he entered her, she moaned and wrapped her legs around his waist. She met every thrust and her nails dug into his back, and when she came, she bit into his shoulder so she wouldn't scream.

Tom came at the same time as his wife. Hearing her fucking with Simon made him shoot almost immediately, and to his surprise, he continue to stay hard after that. He took a quick look at the couple and he could see Simon's cock sliding in and out of his wife's pussy. Instead of stopping, Tom jerked off again and when he came the second time, he simply stood in the corner watching the action.

Simon was ready to come a second time and pulled out of Cindy. He grabbed his cock and let his juices spray over her flat belly and boobs. Then he rolled onto his back next to her.

"Wow, that was something, "she said.

"Yeah, it was. You have such a good pussy, did you know that?"

"No one has ever told me so," she said, increasing her volume to make sure Tom heard it.

Suddenly remembering her dinner appointment, she looked at her watch and then said coldly to Tom, "If you are finished jerking off over there, we have to go."

Tom nodded and went to the bathroom to clean himself. As he was about to close the door, Cindy came in. She put her hands on his cheeks and kissed his lips. "Thank you so much for playing along. I love you very much."

Then she closed the door and Tom was alone, with his still-hard cock.

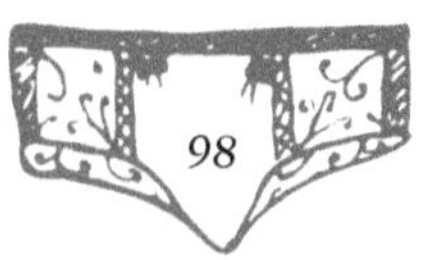

Chapter 14

hen Tom woke up the following morning, he found himself alone in the bed. He lay absolutely still as he looked at the ceiling. His jaws ached slightly and it reminded him of the evening before when he had Simon's cock in his mouth. He felt sick for a second but the feeling of disgust quickly went away. He closed his eyes and brought back the memory of the sounds of his wife being fucked and his cock grew hard. He felt very confused. One part of him hated what had happened, but the other enjoyed it.

He got out of the bed and walked barefooted into the kitchen, expecting to find Cindy making breakfast. It was empty. He then walked to the living room and into the terrace, but she was nowhere to be found. He went back to the kitchen and made some tea. While he waited for the water to boil, he ate a banana and watched the ocean through the window. "It was another day in paradise," he thought, "except that I sucked cock last night." This time, the thought of him going down on Simon didn't make him feel ill and instead, his shaft began to fill with blood. He was shocked as he looked down at his bulging underwear, the sight of it scared him and he began to wonder if he was gay. Shaking his head in horror, he pushed away the thoughts of Simon's cock sliding in and out of his mouth, and focused on making his tea. When it was ready, he took the cup and sat down in the terrace.

"Dude, what's up?"

Tom turned and saw Mike walking up to the bungalow from the beach.

"Not much my friend, can I get you some tea?" muttered Tom.

"No thanks, I'm OK. How are you?"

Tom knew his friend and that he wanted to know how things were going with Simon.

He sighed and put down his cup. "It's OK, I guess. Yesterday was the second night he fucked her."

"Dude, I am so sorry."

"I am getting used to it. Anyway, it's to save the hotel ... so I guess it's for a good cause."

"But still ... having to watch Cindy being fucked can't be much fun?"

"No, it isn't," lied Tom.

In reality, it excited him but he couldn't tell Mike that and he knew that his friend would never be able to understand how he felt and to be honest, neither could he make sense of his own feelings.

"Where is she?"

"I have no idea. I woke up a while ago and she wasn't here. Maybe she went to the market."

"I see."

Mike got up. "Hey, I got to go. The day is still young, there are women to see and pussies to fuck," he said with a laugh.

"Lucky you."

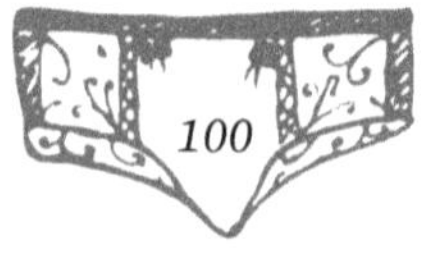

Tom envied Mike at times. The guy had nothing to worry about and lived his life one day at a time. With a sigh, Tom decided to visit his parents as he hadn't seen them in a while.

He walked out through the lobby and when he came to the dirt road, he turned right and followed the off-beaten path up into the hills. After walking for fifteen minutes, he stopped and rested a few minutes before continuing the trek. His parents' place was far away from town. In this part of the island, the air was still and the humidity was oppressing. Tom looked around and saw birds perched on the branches. They were chirping and their songs reminded him of his youth when he and Cindy and their friends used to play hide-and-seek among the trees. He smiled at the memories as he wiped his perspiration off his brow and continue his hike. After walking for another twenty minutes, he came to a clearing at the top of the hill. Right in the middle stood a house made of teak. There were plots of ploughed fields on either side of the house and he quickly spotted a topless man in shorts standing in the fields.

"Hey, Dad!" Tom called out and waved as he made his way across the clearing.

The older man shielded his eyes with his hand. He looked confused for a moment but grinned when he recognized his son.

"Son, what brings you up here?"

"I just wanted to see you and Mom. How are you?"

"The same as always, we are fine. Don't worry about us."

"Where is Mom?"

His father pointed in the direction of the house. "She's inside. Let's go back in."

"Dear, see who has come and visit us," said his father.

The woman sitting by the open fire in the kitchen turned around. Her face broke into a huge smile when she saw Tom. "My baby, it's so nice to see you."

"I have missed you, Mom," said Tom as he hugged her.

"Let me look at my handsome child. How has marriage life been for you? Cindy must be very proud to have you as her husband."

"I hope so."

"Come and sit down. I'll make us some tea."

His mother went back to the stove and put a pot over the fire. She then poured water from a jug into it and added some tea leaves. Tom knew this was a luxury for his parents and that they had to walk half-a-mile every day to get fresh water. As a boy, he had gone to the river several times a day, carrying jugs of water back home.

"How is business at the hotel?" asked his father.

"Good, it is real good actually. The hotel is full and we are expecting it to stay that way through the season."

"That's fantastic! I knew it was worth every penny when I mortgaged the land to pay for your education."

The land the house stood on and most of the hill had belonged to Tom's grandfather and when he died, it was handed down to Tom's father. He had mortgaged it in order to send his only son to the States to further his education. Tom felt horrible and he couldn't bring himself to look his father in his eyes. He hated lying to his parents but there was no way around it.

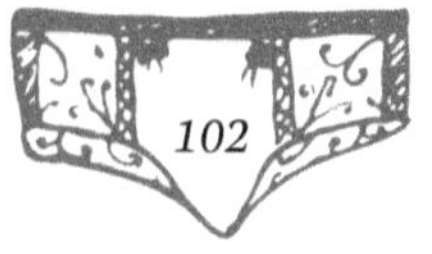

"Are you OK, my son?" asked Tom's mother, sensing something was amiss.

"Yeah, I am just tired. Work is much harder than collage."

The old man chuckled. "And that is nothing compared to working on the land. When I was a boy …."

"Oh, stop it darling. He has heard your stories a thousand times," said Tom's mother as she put a cup of tea in front of her son and another next to her husband.

"And what's wrong with that? It's good for him to hear it again."

"Be quiet, you old man. Son, tell me about Cindy. How is she and when will she come and visit us again?"

"She is fine, it's just that she's very busy with the hotel during this period. As you know, her parents have already moved out from the hotel and there's just too many things for us to handle."

"Like sucking another man's cock in order to keep the place," he thought glumly.

"That's good to know. And when will I be expecting some grandchildren? I am not getting any younger, and it would be nice to be able to hold them before I become too old."

"We are working on it, Mom."

"Well … I know of this special plant that will do wonders to your manhood … make it as hard as a tree trunk. In fact, I have some with me and will pass them to you before you leave," added his father with a wink.

"There is nothing wrong with my manhood, Dad. These things just take time."

Tom chatted with his parents for an hour before leaving.

"Son, are you sure you don't any help?" Tom's dad called after him as began his trek back home.

"No, Dad. I am fine, trust me." Tom answered with a slight tone of annoyance.

The truth is, he wasn't fine at all but he couldn't burden his parents with his problems. All he wanted was to get over and done with this nightmare. There were only two more days left to their agreement with Simon. And then he would pay them what he had promised and leave the island for good. Tom convinced himself that he could hold out for another two days. After all, it was amazing to watch Cindy having an orgasm except that he wasn't the man giving it to her.

Chapter 15

Simon was peeling an orange and watching the news on the TV. The markets were still fluctuating and he couldn't make up his mind as to which stock to put his money on. He had made most of his fortune through real estate investments around the world. When the housing market crashed in Europe and North America in 2008, he had waited a year to make sure it had hit rock bottom before he made his purchases and had invested heavily in villas around the Spanish southern coast and the Balearic Islands.

In the States, he bought properties in Florida and along the California Coast. He then sat back and waited patiently, and it took another two years before the market began its slow and painful recovery. America was the first country to recover from the crash and by 2011, he had sold most of his properties, making a decent profit off them. Even though Spain had yet to recover by then, he decided to refurbish the villas and after a year of renovation works, he had twenty beautiful properties that he rented out for a tidy sum over summer. It was a steady flow of cash into his bank accounts and he sometimes took his wife or a business partner on a vacation to one of these villas.

He ate the peeled orange and used a paper napkin to wipe the juice that spilled from his mouth. He was really enjoying this vacation and everything had been perfect, from the very second he saw Cindy right down to this delicious juicy fruit. Sadly, this was about to come to an end and he would soon have to go back to Hong Kong and a wife who hates oranges.

This evening was the second to last with Cindy, and he was really looking forward to it. She was so tight and firm in the right places and the way she made her husband jump through hoops was hilarious. When she had asked Tom to suck his cock, it was a blast to simply witness the look on the man's face. He must admit though, the young man was a decent cocksucker for a first timer.

There was a knock on the door and Simon got up. He threw the orange peels and napkin in the kitchen's bin, and washed his hands before opening the door.

"Hi," said Cindy as she gave him a peck on the cheek.

Simon was slightly surprised. She had been nervous the last two times and had even avoided shaking his hands and now, she had just given him a kiss. Maybe she was warming up to the situation.

"Hi," he smiled and let the couple in.

Tom was wearing cotton pants and a T-shirt. Cindy was wearing a sleeveless light blue blouse, paired with a short tight skirt that showed off her legs and tight ass. Just like the night before, she wasn't wearing a bra and her little nipples were straining through the fabric.

"Can we have a drink?" she asked sweetly after sitting down in one of the chairs on the terrace.

"Sure, what would you like?"

Cindy gave him a big smile. She then rubbed her hands and said, "A glass of chilled white wine, please."

"How about you, Tom?"

"Whiskey on the rocks, if you have it."

"Single malt?"

"Yes, please."

"All right. "

While Simon was in the kitchen getting the drinks, Cindy leaned forward across the table. "Remember, I love you. You need to know that no matter what happens or what I say, nothing changes the fact that I love you."

Tom nodded his head. They had decided to make the best of things after Cindy had told him how she felt, and Tom had accepted the fact that there was no other way around the situation. She had to fuck Simon and Tom would have to be there for her. After all, he had promised to play along. Moreover, there was no deny he was turned on by what she had asked him to do in the past few nights.

Simon came back with the couple's drinks and placed them on the table.

"What have you guys been up to today?" he asked.

"I visited my parents. They are getting old and I have not seen them for a while," said Tom before taking a sip of his whiskey. When he put down the glass, he said, "This is good. Where did you get it?"

"I bought it in Hong Kong before I flew here. I always bring a bottle of Old Potrero along with me on holidays."

"What about you, Cindy? What did you do?"

"Not much actually. I went for a walk and spent some time with the staff and customers at the hotel. How about you?"

"I went for a swim and sunbathing. There is no place or time for these luxuries in Hong Kong. Damn ... I am so gonna miss this. So, tell me ... how do you find this so far?"

Cindy looked at Tom. "To be honest, Simon, I was looking forward to it. It might sound a bit slutty, but I have come to enjoy our sessions after the past two nights. I like your cock and you are a real gentleman."

"What about you, Tom?" asked Simon.

He sighed. "What can I say? I not entirely pleased with the fact that you are fucking Cindy, but it's not like I can do anything about it. However, I must agree with Cindy that you have been very respectful to the both of us and I appreciate that."

"Cool. And what do you think about sucking my cock last night?"

Tom cleared his throat as he looked away uncomfortably. "Well, it wasn't as bad as I thought it would be."

Simon chuckled. "Yeah, that's what I said after my first time. You know what? I think there is nothing wrong in trying new things and sometimes you might even end up liking it. In my opinion, cock sucking doesn't make one gay as long as you are not attracted to men. Having a friendly blowjob once a year is just child's play."

Tom smiled. Simon's words made sense and he felt a bit better knowing that the man still respected him.

Simon rubbed his hands together and leaned towards Cindy. "Sweetie, I thought we try something different today."

Her eyes widened. "Like what?"

"Anal sex. I would like to fuck that apple-shaped ass of yours and I won't take no for an answer."

"But ..."

"Don't worry. I will be gentle and Tom will be a part of it."

Cindy looked confused. "What do you mean?"

"Well ... for you to be able to relax, I need you to suck Tom's cock and it will take your mind off your ass."

Cindy felt disappointed. Sucking her husband's cock wasn't what she had expected.

"I don't know. I thought it would be just you and me?" she asked reluctantly.

"No, no, we have to include Tom tonight. I think he deserves it after being such a good sport for the last two nights. You don't have to swallow his cum. You just need to play with him as a way of entertaining yourself. Trust me, you will enjoy this."

Tom loved what he was hearing—this was turning into an interesting night. Suddenly he didn't feel as frustrated as before. If Cindy was willing to suck his cock, perhaps there was a chance their sex life could be saved? He gave Cindy a hopeful smile and she returned a half-hearted one.

Cindy was fuming inside as she wondered what Simon was up to. The deal was for Simon to fuck her and not her having to give Tom a blow job. It didn't mean shit when Simon said that she needed to take her mind off the pain that was sure to come when he entered her virgin ass. That was her problem and she could deal with it. What was he up to?

Chapter 16

indy ran her hands run up and down her naked body. She loved the feeling of her round firm boobs and she paused at her nipples, pinching them before moving one hand down to her pussy. She was already wet and her lips were swollen with anticipation.

"You look fantastic, baby," gushed Tom.

He was sitting in his usual chair at the corner of the room and still dressed. But his cock was rock hard in his pants and his eyes were fixed on his wife.

"Oh, shut up. You won't fuck me anyway, so just be quiet."

Tom smiled in acknowledgment—he was getting into the game.

"He is right. You know, you look ravishing and I can't wait to get my hands on you," said Simon who was sitting on the edge of the bed naked. His cock was hard and pre-cum was already slowly oozing out of the tip.

"Thanks, Simon. So, how do we do this?"

"Get on the bed, baby. I'm going to lick your ass and warm you up."

"Mm ... I love the sound of that."

She got on the bed slowly, crawling up like a kitten whilst keeping eye contact with him. She then rested her head on a pillow and pushed her naked ass up in the air. Simon moved in between her legs and spread them so that she could feel his chest against her ass cheeks when she bent down. When his tongue made its first pass over her tight hole, she shivered in pleasure. She closed her eyes and felt his tongue slowly driving her towards the edge of uncontrollable pleasure.

Tom watched and it didn't take long before Cindy started yelping. She moaned and gasped as Simon gave her ass the attention it had never known. At one point, Simon reached out to the nightstand and took a tube of lubricant from the drawer. He squeezed some of the clear gel out of the tube directly on her anus and then dapped his finger on it as he slowly circled the area around before gently probing a finger inside her. Not wanting to miss a second of this spectacular display, Tom inched his chair towards the bed for a closer look.

"Oh, that feels amazing," moaned Cindy.

"I'm glad you like it. I must say, you have a really pretty ass."

"Thanks," she moaned, and then gasped as Simon pressed another finger inside her. The feeling was intense at first, but she began to relax as he slowly slid them in and out of her.

By now, Tom's eyes were wide open in surprise. He couldn't believe his petite wife could take two fingers in her ass without as much as a whimper.

Cindy reached between her legs and found Simon's balls. She massaged them and played with them while she was being finger fucked in the ass. If someone had told her two weeks ago that she would be on all fours and fucked in the ass, she

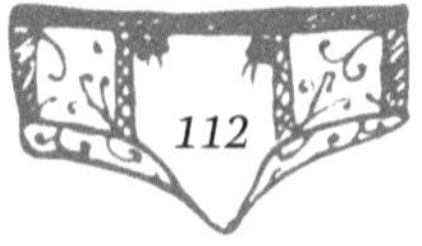

would have told them they were insane, but here she was and loving ever single moment of it. The sensation was so intense and when Simon's other hand moved into her pussy and his finger found her clit, she couldn't hold back and started moaning in sheer pleasure.

"Oh, I want you inside me. Fuck my ass, Simon! Fuck it with that huge cock of yours, please."

Simon chuckled and turned to Tom, "What do you think? Is she ready?"

"I guess so," said Tom, sounding unsure as he was a bit worried that Simon might hurt Cindy.

Taking his cock in one hand, Simon began to lube it up. When he was finally ready, he told Tom in a husky voice, "Guide it in for me."

"OK."

Taking the massive cock in his hand, Tom lined it up with Cindy's asshole and made sure the tip was in the right position. "OK, you can push inside her now." Simon grabbed hold of Cindy's hips while Tom held his cock in place. He began to push it inside her.

Cindy was completely unprepared for the different waves of pain. It began with a flash of pain which became a throbbing dull ache that extended from her ass to every single part of her body. She stopped breathing and closed her eyes, before deciding that she could no longer take it.

"Geez ... take it out, please. Take it out," she winced.

Simon watched Tom, who had a worried look on his face. Then Simon winked at him and pulled out his cock. Cindy let out her breath in a long sigh. She turned her head and looked at him over the shoulder. Her eyes were watery and she spoke quietly.

"That hurts like shit."

"Don't worry, baby. Most women who are doing this for the first time feel the same as you do. It is quite lovely once you get used to it."

She stared at him in disbelief as she wiped a tear from her eye, "Are you sure?"

"Of course, my dear, would I lie to you?"

"No, I guess not, but it really hurts."

"I have an idea."

Simon walked over to the closet and opened his suitcase. He rummaged through the contents before turning around with a big grin on his face and a vibrator in his hand. "Aha! Here you are. Travel tips: Never leave home without a vibrator."

"Let me have a look," said Cindy curiously.

She rolled over on her back and took the vibrator from Simon. It was skin coloured and about seven inches long. It looked like a real cock and felt heavy in her hand. "Must be the batteries," she thought. There was a knob at the base and when she turned it, there was an electric hum. The entire rubber cock began to vibrate in her hand and she smiled.

"Do you like it?" said Simon.

"It looks … interesting."

"You should try it in your pussy, and then in your pretty ass."

She looked confused. "Why? Your cock is perfect for my pussy."

Tom understood where Simon meant and smiled. "Honey, he means that you should use the vibrator in your ass to help you relax, so that you can take him."

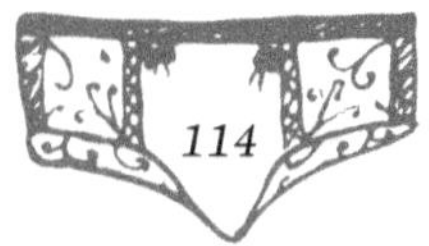

She gave him a look of disgust. "Do you think I am stupid? Of course I know what he meant. You should be quiet or I might use this on your ass," she said wiggling the vibrator in her hand.

"Oh well ..." muttered Tom.

"If you two are finished arguing, maybe we could get back to the fun stuff."

"Sure, I am sorry," said Cindy.

Simon moved in close to her. He helped her roll over on her stomach and then he pulled her ass up towards him. Once she was back in the doggy position, Simon took the vibrator from her and turned it on to a medium speed. Then he slid it in between her legs and let it slide back and forth against her cunt.

"Mm, I like this," purred Cindy.

Tom grinned and gave Simon a thumbs up.

Angling the vibrator a little, Simon pressed its tip against Cindy's clit and the result was immediate. She began to moan and rock back and forth, signaling that she wanted him to slide it inside her. Simon got the message and plunged it inside her wet hole.

"Oh, oh, don't stop, please don't," she moaned.

When she gave the first signs of having an orgasm, Simon took out the vibrator and put the tip against her asshole, allowing her own juices to slide the vibrator in an inch or so. Then he left it in position, buzzing away.

Tom who was sitting just behind Simon watched in amazement as the vibrator slid inside Cindy little by little. Every so often, her ass relaxed a little, and the toy went inside a bit more. Then suddenly, she gave a loud exhalation and her ass opened up as the vibrator slid into base.

"Wow, that was the coolest thing I have ever seen," said Tom.

"What?" Cindy asked.

Tom was confused. Did she not realize that she now had the entire thing in her ass?

"Honey, the vibrator is all the way inside you. Can you feel it?"

"Well, yeah … I guess I can, but there is no real pain, unlike earlier. Right now it more of a dull ache, it's not uncomfortable though."

Simon began to slide the toy in and out of Cindy's butthole and she began to moan even louder.

"That feels so good. Wow, I have never felt anything like it."

"Tom, take off your pants and stand in front of your wife. Cindy, I want you to suck your husband's cock."

Tom got out of the chair excitedly and was naked even before Simon finished his sentence. When he stood in front of Cindy, her eyes had a look he had never seen before. They were unfocused and there was almost a dream-like quality in them. It took her a while to register that her husband was standing in front of her and that he had angled his cock downwards for her to take it in her mouth. As if snapping back to reality, she looked at him unhappily.

"Don't get used to this. I am only doing it because Simon asked me to."

At this point in time, Tom didn't care what his wife said. He was just happy to finally have his cock sucked. He closed his eyes and sighed in pleasure as Cindy's lips slowly slid over his cockhead and down along the shaft until she reached the base.

She ran her tongue over and under his cockhead and that brought a moan from him. She was supporting her own weight with her hands and couldn't touch Tom cock. Instead, she continued to bob her head up and down the best she could.

Seeing that Cindy was getting accustomed to have the vibrator in her, Simon waited for the right moment to swop the toy with his now bulging penis and pushing it into her sweet hole.

"Argh," groaned Cindy in pain as Simon applied more pressure inside her.

"Sh ... darling, just relax."

"Unhhh ..."

Simon began to thrust in and out of her gently, pushing only half way in. He moved in a steady rhythm and he felt her muscles relaxed as her sweet ass beckoned him to go deeper inside. Sensing that Cindy was ready, he dropped the vibrator on the bed, grabbed her hips with both hands and increased the force of his thrusts.

Cindy closed her eyes as she clenched her fists. She couldn't believe she was being fucked in the ass by a monster cock. What had just seemed impossible a few minutes ago was taking place and on top of that, it dawned upon her that she was actually enjoying sucking Tom's cock. It was rock hard and her jaws didn't ache like how they were when she went down on Simon. Her husband's cock was perfect for her lips. She began to bob her head up and down fervently and before she knew it, he came. She struggled to swallow once ... twice ... three times before he shuddered and pulled out of her.

"Wow, honey! That was amazing. Thank you so much," he grinned.

She didn't answer and gave him a brief smile instead as she started panting. By now, Simon had increased the tempo as well as depth of his thrusts.

"Tom, quit staring. Come over here and give me a hand." Simon handed him the vibrator and instructed, "Take this and slide it into her pussy, then fuck her with it."

Tom picked up the toy and when he was about to insert it inside Cindy, Simon whispered, "When I pull out of her ass, I want you to slide in between her legs and lick her pussy while you fuck her with the vibrator."

Tom didn't answer, but nodded and grinned like a little boy. This was a completely different session from the past few nights. He was enjoying it immensely and hoped that his wife felt the same way too.

Simon then focused on pounding Cindy as he watched for the signs and made sure that he timed everything perfectly. He gave Tom a nod and pulled out from Cindy the moment she started gasping and writhing.

Cindy, on the other hand, was feeling a sudden emptiness where a world of pleasure had been before. She was confused until she felt something warm and soft attached to her clit. She looked down between her legs and saw her husband sucking eagerly on her while sliding the vibrator in and out of her now swollen pussy.

"What the ..." she started to swear, but Simon cut her off.

"Shh. Just enjoy it darling. Don't say another word."

Cindy was about to push Tom away when she felt a wave of sensations flowing through her pussy. She gasped and then shuddered as the orgasm ripped through her body. The intense feeling of Tom's lips and tongue against her clit was just too much to bear. She began to moan and held her breath, before

finally collapsing on top of Tom as he slowly slid the soaking vibrator out of her pussy.

Lying under his wife and with her hot cunt still pressed against his face, Tom had a big grin on his face. The happiness he felt was close to euphoria. Even though Simon had done most of the work, he was the one who had made his beautiful hot wife come. He wiggled out from under Cindy and sat on the floor with the vibrator still humming in his hand. Simon patted his back and went out of the bedroom before coming back with two glasses of whiskey in his hands.

"Here you go. Well done!" he handed Tom one glass and sipped from the other.

Tom drained the whiskey in one big gulp and then placed the empty glass on the floor next to him. "Thank you, Simon. Thank you for letting me do that."

"Oh, it was nothing. I am just glad you eventually did it."

"What, guys?" Cindy was smiling in bliss as she looked at the two men from the bed. Then as if she had just been rudely awakened from a dream, she pointed at Tom and glared at him. "What are you guys talking about? And who gave you permission to eat my cunt?!" she demanded.

"I did, and you should have let him do it earlier."

"He is useless in bed."

With a sigh, Simon placed his half empty glass on the bedside table and then sat down on the bed. He took Cindy's head and put in his lap as she sobbed. He then gently stroked her back. "No, honey, he is not useless. The problem is that you have no patience. I know you love each other, but that is not

119

enough to make good sex. It's not even remotely close. You have to explore it together and not assume that Tom knows everything."

Cindy sniffed as she lifted her head and looked Simon in the eyes. "You don't understand. He is the impatient one. All he ever does is to stick his pathetic cock inside me and fuck me like a rabbit."

Simon chuckled and looked at Tom, who was now looking offended. "Maybe you are right, but that's why it is so important to communicate with each other."

Cindy pushed Simon away angrily. She then stomped into the bathroom and locked the door. Tom was about to go after her, but Simon stopped him. "Wait and just let her be. She needs some time to think it through."

"Some time for? I love her and I want to be with her. It hurts me to see my wife upset."

Simon tried to be as patient as he could. "My friend, she needs time to think about what I told her, and you need time to cool down. And just because you made her come tonight, it doesn't mean that you will be able to do the same tomorrow, remember that."

"OK, you are right."

"You know what? Go back and take a shower. Then call Mike and go out for some drinks. I'm going to talk to Cindy alone."

Tom looked reluctant. He didn't like the idea of leaving Cindy alone with Simon and his big and still erect cock.

"No, Simon. You don't know her ..."

"Don't worry and leave. I promise nothing will happen."

"Fine, but please respect the fact that I am her husband."

"Yes, I do."

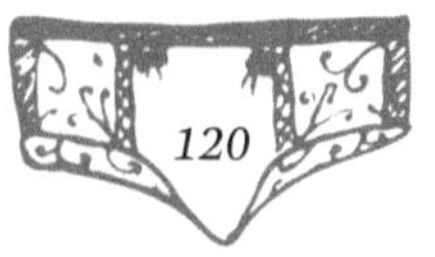

Tom walked out of the bedroom and grabbed his clothes along the way. He then made his way back to the bungalow and took a hot shower before calling Mike, who was at an infamous titty bar downtown. With a sigh, Tom wrote a note for Cindy, saying that he missed her and pleaded for her not to be angry with him. He then put it on her pillow and left to meet Mike.

Chapter 17

indy was fuming under the hot shower. How could Simon do that to her? That wasn't part of the deal they had made and only she could order Tom around. He was her husband and now Simon had taken it upon himself to have Tom touch her. Not only that, he had told him to lick her pussy!

She rinsed the shampoo out from her hair and then turned off the water. She took a towel from a hanger on the back of the door and quickly dried herself.

There was water running down her legs when she opened the bathroom door and stepped into the bedroom, expecting to see her husband and Simon. To her surprise, it was empty apart from the faint smell of sex and sweat lingering in the air. Scanning the room, she saw the vibrator lying on the floor where Tom had dropped it. She picked it up and smiled at the memory of the immense pleasure it had brought her. She then put it down on the bedside table and went looking for the two men.

She found Simon sitting naked on the terrace with a bottle of water in one hand and a cigar in the other.

"Have you calmed down?" he asked.

She didn't answer. Instead she sat down opposite him and reached for the bottle of water. She drained it in two long gulps before putting the empty bottle on the table.

"I'll get another," Simon got up and went into the kitchen.

When he came back, Cindy was sitting on the railing and looking out over the calm sea. She turned towards him and said accusingly, "You had no right to do that."

He smiled at her. "I had every right. Remember our deal? During the days that I am with you, I have the right to everything that has to do with your body and tonight, I wanted to watch your husband lick your pussy until you came, so deal with it."

She scowled and turned her face away from him. He shrugged his shoulders and continued smoking his cigar. It took another five minutes before she finally spoke.

"What did you mean when you said that we were not giving each other the opportunity?"

Simon watched the beautiful woman for a minute before answering. "Tell me something, Cindy. Have you ever been with another man apart from Tom? And don't lie ... I have slept with enough women to know the truth."

Cindy's mind went back to the night with Klaus in the kitchen. She sighed and then whispered in guilt, "Yes, but we didn't fuck. I just sucked his cock once."

Simon didn't say anything and simply nodded slowly.

Cindy was confused. Was he upset with her? Was he judging her? "What? Talk to me, Simon."

"Was the other man experienced?"

"I guess. I don't think he was as experienced as you are, but definitely a lot more than Tom."

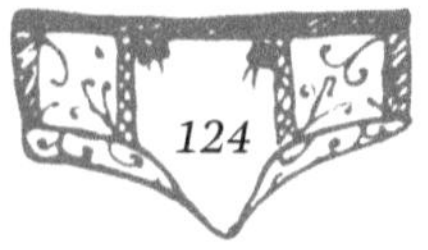

124

"Mm, I see. Has it ever crossed your mind that because of that one encounter, you expect all men to know what to do for you to come?"

Cindy blushed. "Don't be stupid. Of course not."

"OK, then explain the frustration you have with Tom's lack of experience."

"Well ... he is unable to give me the pleasure I want and I can't help but feel this way."

"Bullshit. You can give him a chance—a chance to learn together, to explore each other and having fun while you do it. No one is born a great lover, you have to learn it."

Cindy scoffed. "Exactly! Tom doesn't know what he is doing. He sticks his dick inside me, humps for about thirty seconds, and then it's over."

"And how would you like it then?"

She was quiet for a while, and finally answering, "Like the way you do it."

"Thanks honey, but I have been fucking around since I was a teenager, while Tom was a virgin when you slept with each other on your wedding night."

"So?"

"How can you compare a virgin to a guy like me? It's not fair for him, is it?"

Cindy put her hands to her face and began sobbing. Simon got up and sat down on the railing next to her. He put an arm around her shoulder and hugged her close. "C'mon, it's OK. Dry your tears and I'll make us something to eat."

She nodded as he left her and walked back into the kitchen to prepare some eggs and a fruit salad.

"Look at those boobs, man," said Mike, pointing at the young woman dancing around the pole in the middle of a raised platform.

"Silicone tits," laughed Tom as he took another drink from his mug.

"I don't give a shit, they can be made with old tires for all I care, but damn, she looks hot."

Tom watched the girl for a while and then looked around for the waitress. He made eye contact and signaled for another round of drinks. Their table was full of empty bottles and shot glasses. When the drinks arrived, he and Mike clinked glasses and swept their shots, guzzling them down with beer.

Tom hadn't been this drunk since his university days. It felt like eons when in fact, it had only been a few months that he had left the States. So much had happened since then: he had gotten married to his childhood sweetheart and became an owner of a resort. And now he was on the verge of losing everything. His wife preferred another man's cock, and he was getting drunk in a cheap titty bar.

He thought of his wife naked in Simon's room and on her knees and elbows being fucked by the monster cock, and suddenly had the urge to go back and be with her. He tapped Mike's shoulder and his friend turned around. "What?"

"I'm going home. I will get the bill before I leave."

"C'mon, my friend, stay for a while longer. The fun hasn't even started."

"No, I've got to go."

Tom got up and made his way towards the bar on wobbly legs. He found some bills in his pocket and put them on the bar

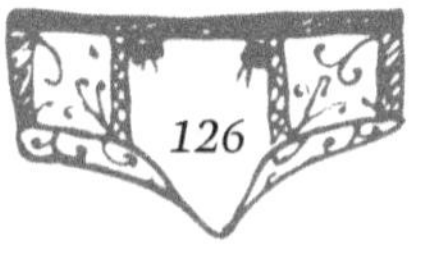

table, making sure the waitress saw them. Then he made his way back home.

The red light district was full of dodgy tourists hunting for hot young bodies, and girls looking for fat wallets. Pausing twice to puke, he felt like a tourist. No self respecting Thai would ever vomit in public, but he didn't give a shit right now with his life in the dumps. Tom ran the last couple of yards back to the hotel and almost tripped over himself when he made his way past the reception. He waved the young receptionist away when she stepped out from behind the desk to help him back on his feet.

When he reached the bungalow, he saw that the lights were on. "Fucking asshole. He had better not be fucking Cindy inside our house," he thought. He slammed open the front gate and stormed inside.

"Where are you, bastard?" he roared.

He went to the bedroom, expecting to find Simon and his naked wife in bed. It took him a while for his eyes to adjust to the darkness. He heard a slight whimper and a click as Cindy turned on the light.

"What happened?" asked Cindy sleepily.

"Where is he?"

"Who?"

"Simon, I know he is here. I knew he would fuck you when I wasn't around."

Cindy sighed. "Honey, you are drunk. Come to bed. Simon is asleep in his room."

"What? But ..."

"Shush, darling. We can talk in the morning when you are feeling better."

Heaving a sigh of relief, Tom crept under the sheets next to Cindy. He put an arm over her and snuggled close.

"You reek of booze."

"Sorry."

"It's okay. I love you. Let's get some sleep."

"OK."

Chapter 18

The next morning, Cindy stood over the bed and looked down at her snoring husband. He was asleep on his back with his arms and legs spread out. His mouth was slightly ajar and there was a foul smell coming out of it.

She sipped some of the coffee from her mug and then nudged him, "Wake up, baby."

There was no response so she sat down on the floor and put the coffee mug close to his nose. He stirred a little before turning over on his side.

Tom was not a coffee drinker but she thought he might just need it today.

"C'mon, wake up."

"Uh huh," he murmured with his eyes closed.

"I know you can hear me and just so you know, I don't feel sorry for you at all. I guess it turned out to be quite a night with Mike."

Tom grudgingly turned towards her and licked his parched lips. "It feels like I have sandpaper in my mouth."

"Here's some coffee for you."

"No, thank you. Would you please bring me some water?"

She smiled at him. "No, get up and get it yourself. I will see you in the kitchen."

Tom slowly moved his legs over the side of the bed until he felt the floor under his feet. He stood up very slowly and attempted to get his drink from the kitchen, but barely made it beyond two steps when his stomach turned over and he had to run to the bathroom.

"Damn ... I will never do that again," he stumbled into the kitchen ten minutes later.

"Do what, drink?"

"Yeah. But more specifically, shots with Mike."

"Where did you go?"

He gave her the name of the titty bar and she laughed, "That's pretty much where I'd expect to find Mike—the home of the 'shaved pussy shots'."

"Please don't remind me about that dodgy place."

"All right. Honey, will you come and sit down at the table? We need to talk."

Sensing the change in the tone of her voice, Tom walked up to her in concern. "Are you OK? I mean ... you were quite upset last night."

She kissed his cheek. "I'm fine. Simon and I had a long talk after you left."

Tom pulled back slightly in surprise. "Talk?"

"Yeah, what were you expecting?"

"Nothing much. And what did you talk about?"

"Sex."

"And do I really need to listen to this?"

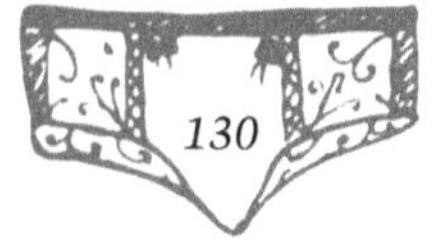

130

"You won't have to. I guess I will show you tonight. And now, we have other things to discuss."

He sat down at the kitchen table as Cindy gave him the mug of coffee she had prepared earlier. He drank some of it and smiled at her. "This is not too bad, I already feel better."

"That's the magic of coffee. Tomorrow, Simon will give us a check for the two hundred thousand that we owe the bank. We need to pay off the debt as soon as possible and get back to serious business in the hotel. The season is picking up and we have had enough games these last few days."

"Some had more fun than others," grunted Tom.

"Oh, stop it. We agreed to do this together. Besides, all this will be over tomorrow. Now, cheer up and let's spend some time at the beach before things get busy."

While Cindy packed some towels and a bottle of suntan lotion into her bag, Tom went to the reception to make sure everything was running smoothly. He then did his usual rounds and greeted the customers. He spotted Simon on his terrace and waved to him. Simon waved back as he pointed at the phone he was holding to his ear.

Soon after, Cindy met Tom outside their bungalow and they made their way across the hot sand towards the edge of the water. There was a small crowd lounging at the area in front of the hotel. Some of them were the hotel's guests and the others were tourists from the surrounding resorts that did not have a proper beach bar.

After combing the area for a while, the young couple found the perfect spot to lay their towels down and soak up the sun.

"So this is how it feels like to be a tourist," said Tom.

"I guess so. It's a pretty good feeling, don't you think?"

Tom lifted his head and watched two young women in their skimpy bikinis coming out of the water a few yards away. "Yeah, it sure is."

"Quit ogling at the women and help me with the lotion."

Cindy rolled over on her stomach and Tom shifted so he was sitting next to her. He poured some of the cream on her back and began to massage it into her skin. She was a shade lighter than he was and had to take extra precautions to make sure her skin didn't burn in the sun.

"Thanks, baby. That feels so good … I think I'm going to take a nap," she murmured.

"And I'll keep watch over you, so no one takes my beautiful wife away."

Tom bent down and kissed her neck, before laying back down on the towel and closing his eyes as he soaked up the sun.

Chapter 19

After a light dinner, Cindy went to the bedroom to get ready for the evening with Simon while Tom did the dishes. He was drying the dishes when she walked into the kitchen dressed in a pair of denim shorts and a simple white T-shirt.

"You look good," he whistled.

"Thanks, baby. Simon told me he had a surprise for us tonight, I wonder what it is."

"Another vibrator perhaps?" said Tom as he winked at her.

Cindy giggled. "Maybe, I wonder what it would feel like to have one in my ass and one in my pussy."

"That sounds kinky and I would love to see it."

"I bet you would. C'mon, finish drying the dishes so you can get ready. I'll wait for you outside."

Outside, the night was calm and the stars shone bright in the black sky. Cindy took off her shoes and let the sand trickle between her toes. It was still warm from the hot afternoon sun and felt soft on her skin. She heard Tom lock the front gate and he made his way down the steps to where she was standing.

"Ready?" he asked.

"Yeah, and just so you know, I will always love you no matter what happens tonight."

"And I you."

He took her hand and they began the short walk to Simon's bungalow.

"Welcome lovebirds, how was your day?" smiled Simon, when he opened the door.

"Fine. How about yours?" asked Cindy cheerfully.

"Busy. I'm going home tomorrow and I need to prepare for some business meetings that I'd need to attend once I arrive in Hong Kong."

The trio walked out to the terrace where a bottle of wine was chilling in an ice bucket. Cindy and Tom made themselves comfortable on the bamboo sofa as Simon sat opposite them.

"So, this is our last night together. I told Cindy yesterday that I have a surprise for you."

"What is it?" asked Tom as he poured pouring the wine into the glasses.

Simon said as he glanced deliberately at Cindy, "Only Tom will be fucking you tonight, and I'll be watching."

"What?" blurted Cindy with a clear tone of surprise and disappointment in her voice.

"It's time you learn about each other and I will be there to guide you."

Tom's heart skipped a beat. Had he heard this right? Was he finally going to fuck Cindy?

"What if I don't, you know, come?" said Cindy, concerned.

Simon smiled at her and lifted his glass. "You will and I am sure of it. Let's make a toast to the first Tom-Cindy orgasm."

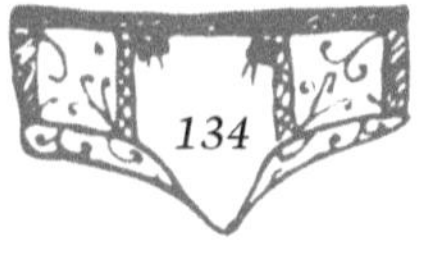

Tom's excitement ebbed as he realized what was expected of him. He knew he couldn't hold out for more than a few minutes before blowing his load, while Cindy needed time to climax. He prayed silently to all the sex gods that had ever existed that he would be able to hold back this time round.

They took their time to finish their wine as Simon told the young couple about some of his ongoing investments. When their glasses were empty, he led an anxious Tom and a very apprehensive Cindy into the bedroom.

"Here we are, the moment of truth has arrived. This is not a time to be skeptical or egocentric. Instead you should learn to enjoy each other."

Cindy and Tom looked at each other and then at Simon.

"What are you waiting for? Get naked, guys," he instructed.

They slowly undressed and Simon immediately saw that Cindy wore a white thong under her shorts. She had not worn any underwear during the last couple of nights. He knew that she chose to go braless and was able to see her nipples pushing against the fabric out on the terrace earlier. His cock stirred at the display of beautiful flesh in front of him, but he had promised himself to behave tonight. After all, he had had plenty of her fine body over the last few nights.

"OK, good. Get on the bed and I'll explain what you need to do."

Tom's cock had already become rock hard and when Cindy saw it, she felt that special buzz in her stomach. It made her smiled—she was becoming horny and it was her husband who was now making her feel this way.

"What's so funny?" asked a bewildered Tom as he stepped out of his Bermuda shorts.

"Nothing, dear, it's all good."

Tom got onto the bed and lay down. He wasn't sure what to expect and it made him nervous. The fact that Simon sat in the chair which he usually occupied didn't make things better. In fact, it felt really strange and awkward to him. When he had been the observer, his cock had been hard right from the beginning of every session and now, he looked down at his flaccid member and panicked. Simon must have seen the worried look on his face because he gave the young man an air fist bump and said, "Don't worry. You'll have a hard-on even before you know it."

A reluctant Cindy took her time to get on the bed and lay down next to her husband. His limp cock put her off and she didn't feel the least bit comforted when Simon said, "Tom moved in between Cindy's legs and lick her pussy." After all, what did he know? Her husband had no skill and all he was capable of was lapping at her clit and lips with no technique or whatsoever.

Tom spread Cindy's legs gently with his hands and lay down on his stomach so his head was above her pussy. Then he stuck out his tongue and pressed it against her clit.

"No, that is wrong. You have to lick around it and let your tongue flicker over it," Simon said patiently.

Tom tried again as he took heed of Simon's instructions and Simon tapped his shoulder reassuringly, "This is much better. Keep doing that while keeping an eye on Cindy's reaction."

Cindy didn't feel anything much at the beginning apart from the sensation of husband's wet and warm tongue against her pussy but as minutes passed, a comfortable tickling feeling began

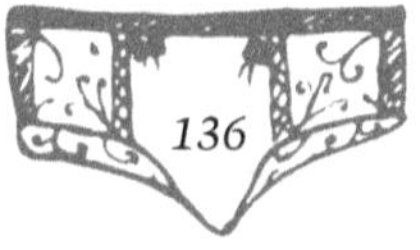

to spread from between her legs. She squirmed a little and a deep sigh of pleasure escaped her mouth as she smiled. Tom lifted his head for a second and saw that his wife had a look of pure joy on her face. The sight of this was a huge encouragement and he went back to flicker her sweet spot.

Cindy couldn't believe it—Tom was actually getting the hang of it. The tingling feeling had now turned into waves of deep pleasure. She began to press her pussy against his lips, and could hear Tom lapping up the pussy juice from between her legs as she became wet.

"Oh god, you are so wet," grinned Tom.

"Shh ... keep going, honey. This feels fantastic," she moaned.

Simon watched the couple from the chair and nodded in approval as it became clear all is not lost for the young couple. Tom was doing a great job, all things considered, and Cindy was responding to his efforts. When she finally took hold of his Tom's head and pressed him against her dripping cunt, Simon knew she was ready for the next part.

"Cindy, I want you to get on top of Tom so the both of you are in a sixty-nine position."

When they had shifted positions, Simon continued. "All right, now listen carefully, Cindy. Tom comes very quickly so you can't blow him too hard. Instead, focus on maintaining his erection."

Tom looked down at his hard cock when he heard the word "erection", he smiled in relief. He hadn't even noticed it, but he had become hard while licking Cindy and hearing her moans.

"Tom, while you continue to lick Cindy, wet one finger and slide it in and out of her ass. She loves that," added Simon.

Looking at Tom, Cindy slowly lowered her lips until they touched the tip of Tom's cock. She could taste the pre-cum as she stuck out her tongue and licked around his cockhead. The tangy taste excited her and she took all of his cock in her mouth, savouring the hard shaft.

"Slowly, honey ... or I will come," warned Tom.

Nodding in acknowledgment, she took his cock out of her mouth and began to lick the shaft up and down, before turning her attention to his balls. He started moaning and she continued pleasing him with her mouth, making sure she didn't get close to the sensitive parts.

Tom couldn't believe it. His wife had just deep-throated him and it was the best feeling ever. Not even Melanie, that professional cocksucker had done that to him. He looked at his wife's hairless pussy that was mere inches from his face, then grabbed her hips and pulled her down to his level so that his mouth could access her cunt. He sucked on her swollen clit with a fervour and let his tongue dance around and over it. He then slid his middle finger into her soaked pussy and smiled as he felt her muscles tighten around it. He slowly pulled out and gently inserted his now juice covered finger into her asshole. Her reaction was immediate.

"Oh, wow! That is awesome."

He began to fingerfuck her ass while continuing to lick her clit. Unable to control herself, Cindy began to ride his finger whilst slapping her dripping pussy into his face; he was loving every single second of it.

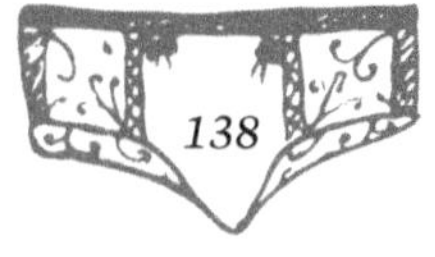

By now, Cindy was so horny that she wanted Tom's cock inside her pussy. She had never expected Tom would be able to make her feel the way she felt right now.

"Oh, baby ... I want you to fuck me," she moaned.

"What are you waiting for? Let her ride you," urged Simon.

Tom got out from under Cindy and she turned around so she was facing him. She then slid up so her legs were wrapped around his body and his cock was under her pussy. Without a moment's hesitation, she grabbed his hard dick and guided it inside her.

"Woah ... woah ... woah. You are so hot and so incredibly wet," he licked his lips as he looked at her.

"All thanks to you, baby and I love you for it."

As Cindy began to ride him, he put his hands on her firm boobs and massaged them slowly. Her nipples were hard against his palms and when he pinched them, she moaned louder.

Back on the chair, Simon was crossing his finger that Tom could hold his erection for a few minutes longer. When Cindy finally threw back her head and began to gasp, he knew she was close to coming.

What had been a warm fuzzy feeling in her cunt suddenly extended to every part of her body. She thrashed her head from side to side and pressed her thighs against her husband, before closing her eyes and moaned as the orgasm ripped through her.

Tom's cock was now deep within Cindy's pussy and it gripped on tightly. As she continued to ride him, an orgasm grew in his balls. He gasped a few times before letting out a groan as his semen eventually exploded out of his shaft and into her. Cindy's thighs

finally let up a little as their juices mixed and she fell on top of him, breathing hard in his ear.

Simon stood up and smiled. "That was incredible."

Looking up, Cindy looked at the older man and managed a weak smile. She turned her face and watched her husband's face. It was calm and he had a big smile on his lips.

"That was amazing," she whispered.

"Yeah, it was, wasn't it?"

"You made me come, honey."

"Yes, I did."

Cindy pushed herself up with her arms and looked down at her now exhausted husband. She kissed him on the mouth, and their tongues were soon entwined in a playful tug-of-war. Tom put his arms around her and they rolled over so he was on top. He then slid his still-hard cock into her.

"Can you do it again?" she asked with hunger in her voice.

"Yes, because you make me so hot, baby," he said while thrusting in and out of her.

Cindy adjusted herself so his cock rubbed against her clit whilst it slid its way into her hot pussy, and within seconds she began to feel another orgasm growing inside her. She wrapped her legs around his waist and pulled him closer.

Tom kissed her and fucked her until she came. She bit him so hard on the shoulder while writhing in pleasure from her orgasm. He knew it would leave a mark but he didn't care. When he was about to come, he pulled out and jerked off so his hot semen landed on her boobs and belly.

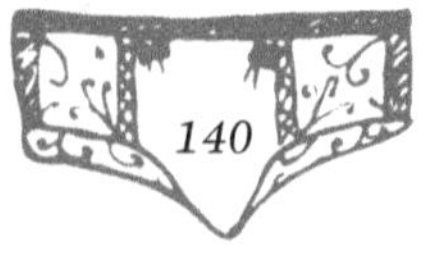

"Wow, that was quite a lot for a second time," said Cindy as she looked down at her tits and smiled.

"Honey, I have watched Simon fuck you for days and this builds up"

She giggled and pulled him close. "I love you. Let's take a shower and join Simon outside."

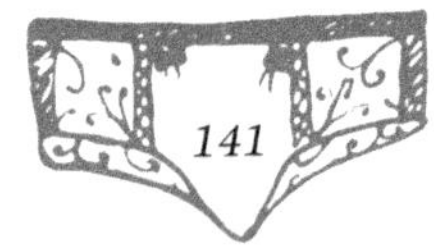

Chapter 20

The beaming couple walked out to terrace where Simon was finishing his second glass of whiskey. "We would like to thank you for your help," said Cindy.

They were now sitting down on the sofa and as Simon opened another bottle of wine.

"No problem. I'm happy I could help."

"I think you have saved our marriage," said Tom.

Simon laughed. "I certainly hope so. You are a great couple and I had a wonderful time with you." Pointing to a small white envelope on the table, he said, "In the envelope is a check for the amount we agreed upon. I am leaving early tomorrow morning and I guess I won't be seeing you for a while."

Cindy picked up the envelope and slipped it into her pocket without opening it. She trusted Simon and knew that he was a man of his word. "Thank you, Simon. It has been a long night. We will make a move first so you can get some rest. Please keep in touch."

Cindy gave Simon a hug and kissed him on the cheeks, and Tom shook his hand. The couple held hands as they made their back to their bungalow. As they were about to step inside, Cindy said, "Let's going over to my parents' and tell them we have the money."

"Hi, Mom. How are you?"

"I'm fine, baby. How about you? Are you all right?"

"Great, we've finally raised enough money to pay the bank."

Her mother laughed, "That's fantastic! How did you do it?"

Cindy was quiet as she wasn't sure what to reply but finally replied, "We borrowed it from one of Tom's friends in the States. We've promised to return him the money once the hotel's finances are back in shape."

"Well ... you didn't need to."

Cindy was confused. "What? What do you mean?"

"We have the money."

"But a few days ago, you said ..."

"We just wanted to see how you would solve the problem. Call Tom's friend and tell him you don't need the money. Good night, honey. It's pretty late now and I've just taken my medicine. I'm feeling a bit under the weather. Why don't we speak more tomorrow?"

Cindy stood dumbfounded on the steps. Her head was spinning as she struggled to make sense of the situation. Tom, who was busy with a guest who needed some help earlier, caught up with her. He immediately sensed that something was amiss.

"Are you all right? How are your parents?"

She didn't answer.

"Baby? What happened?"

She turned around slowly and said, "They had the money."

"What money? I don't understand."

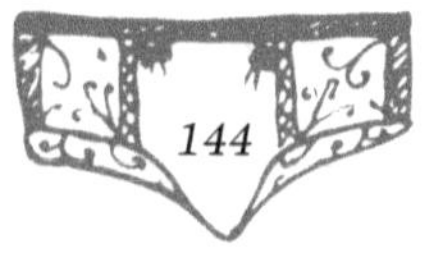

"My parents had the money all along. They just wanted to see if we were capable of running the hotel and find out how important the hotel meant to us."

"Damn. So all that we have done ... well, you have done with Simon was for nothing?"

She put her hands on his shoulders and stepped in close. Cindy's lips brushed against his and she whispered. "No, baby, it was for everything. Now we know we are perfect for each other. You can make me come and I adore you for it."

Tom grinned. "Let's go back home. I'm feeling horny right now."

She kissed him and whispered in his ear. "Let's fuck until the bank opens. I want you inside me all night."

Simon walked past the young couple's bungalow while on his way to the reception the next day and smiled when he heard Cindy's unmistakable moans of pleasure. He was sure that he would have this woman's sweet pussy again, and had no doubt she'll be well-satisfied by her husband till then.